Thor's Dragon Rider
Book Three

ENTRAPMENT

"Kara the wingless Valkyrie and her beloved dragon companion, Elan, find themselves in deep trouble once more. Stuck in a swelteringly hot realm of molten rock and fire, they are outmatched and isolated. *Entrapment* is a claustrophobic roller-coaster ride for fans of the series!" Kelly R., Line Editor, Red Adept Editing

Hoodwinked

To my readers - I'd like to apologise for the cliffhanger in the last book… right after the apology I receive from all the other books and TV series that left me hanging off the edge, begging for more.

BLURB

Protecting friends is deadly.

It's happened. Hel has sent her minion to attack Asgard, or so Kara thought. She and Elan are entrapped and dragged into the depths of Muspelheim, the land of the fire giants, bringing a whole new meaning to "warm welcome."

In an attempt to retrieve the information Kara holds, creatures that live only in nightmares surface, threatening Kara's freedom and life.

Chapter One

Elan's golden scales crush against my chest as the lava monster's grasp tightens, squeezing us together against its palm. Extending my body is a struggle as I'm pressed flat against her scales. I have just enough room to gaze over my shoulder and peer through a crack between the dark digits.

The finger cage traps in the heat, raising the circulating temperature. Sweat breaks out on my brow and trickles into my eye. The hard surface of the lava monster's skin is warm from internal heating. Combined with the stress pumping adrenaline through my veins, it makes the enclosure almost as hot as a sauna.

A soft puff of colder breeze sneaks through the crack as I observe our surroundings, my mind racing to find a way out.

The scenery changes, and my stomach flops to my torso floor, only to rebound, tightening into a knot as an eye of red lava stares at the hand confining us. I let my magic well up. Having had no luck against the frost giants, I don't know how to combat this monstrous beast. The lava monster is just as big as the frost giants and maybe more vicious. I don't know how we're going to get out of this predicament.

"How are you feeling, Elan?" My voice is muffled against the large hand.

A little squashed. But I'm fine, other than it's my worst nightmare come true. I don't understand why it's not attacking us. It's just grabbing us. Even though her voice is internal, speaking directly into my mind, it still sounds strained. That's probably because of the pressure against her head. *How are you feeling?*

"My heart's pumping a hundred miles per hour, and the heat is causing me to sweat. I can feel it gathering in the leather down my thighs." I attempt to shift my hands to rub my legs, only to find I can hardly move them. "Other than that and being cramped, I'm fine."

Observing what little I can through the crack, I attempt to work out where we are.

"It's weird for it to be just grabbing us." An itch grows on my stomach, and I'm desperate to scratch it, with no success. "Why would Hel be targeting us? If anything, we should be safe because I accidentally let Loki go."

The hand tightens, and Elan groans. *I don't know. It doesn't make sense.*

The hand loosens slightly, and I suck in the fresh air. "Do you have any ideas on how to get out of here?"

Nope. I have no idea. She squirms to get comfortable, only to press me farther.

I grunt. "Stop moving! You're squashing me."

Her body goes deathly still. *Sorry.* Her chest expands a couple of times as she takes some breaths. *Except for the massive horn sticking out of its head, it's much like the lava monster from earlier that injured me badly.*

Slightly shifting my head enables me to see somewhat more through the crack, and I catch a brief glimpse of the monster's face. Glowing red-and-orange lava fills gaping holes resembling eyes. As I gaze into them, the sensation of death assails me. I worry my lip but halt when a flash of lightning fills the sky behind the monster's head. A booming clap of thunder reverberates the surrounding area only seconds later.

My heart skips a beat. "Is that one of Thor's electrical storms?"

Another flash of lightning forks through the sky.

I don't know, but I sure hope it is.

Something thuds. Suddenly, we jerk to one side

before being overcome by a strange feeling of floating on air, still enclosed within the giant hand. I peer out the crack, attempting to focus on the land streaking past.

The giant hits the ground with a thud, and the fist holding us slams against the solid surface. The impact reverberates through my body, banging my body harder against Elan's scales before slapping me against the palm.

The sliver of a crack between its clenched fingers opens wider. I peer out in time to see the ground bounce underneath us, and something careens through the sky. Focusing on the flying object, I see Mjolnir charging through the air and landing right back in Thor's hands.

I gasp. "It is Thor!"

He stands with his feet splayed shoulder distance apart as he releases Mjolnir again and braces for the hammer's impact, and his shoulder jerks backward when it slams back into his hand.

I can see. Excitement fills Elan's voice.

My breath catches as he launches the hammer at the giant, bracing for another hit. His movements are so fluid and quick that the giant doesn't have time to rise to its feet. Even so, the impact flings the giant lava monster across the ground, the hand around us refusing to release its grip.

Mjolnir yanks free from the giant's abdomen, returning at Thor's call, the head of the hammer glowing golden red as though it had been embedded in a fiery lava pit. The color changes back to silver as the metal cools before it slams back into Thor's hand. The hammer must've gone straight through the lava monster to make it glow like that. I'm astonished that the lava monster is still clasping us.

A strange groan fills the air, and the monster's body shudders as it rises to its feet. In a muffled and unnatural voice that's barely decipherable, it says, "I have no quarrel with you, Thor, God of Thunder. I'm not attacking Asgard. There is no reason for your attack on me."

With his hammer raised and feet splayed, ready for a fight, Thor narrows his eyes. "Besides being on Asgard without invitation, you have captured my Valkyrie and her dragon. This action alone has instantly made you my enemy."

The giant releases a displeased grunt. "I will not release this Valkyrie and dragon." The monster bends low, releasing words filled with determination that sound like they are being gargled through a bubbling lava stream. "I must return with this Valkyrie and her companion. It's my command to do so or not to return at all."

Thor pulls the raised hammer back, his voice

deep and loud as he matches the monster's intensity. "Then you shall not return at all." His shoulder thrusts forward as he releases the hammer straight at the lava monster's face.

My heart skips with hope and ripples with cheer, thankful that Thor is on my side. Unsuccessfully, I attempt to clap my squashed hands as the hammer careens straight for the monster's face.

Disappointment grips me when the monster jerks, and Thor's face twists with disappointment. The beast must have shifted its head to the side, causing Mjolnir to miss. The lack of any jarring fuels my assumption.

Quickly, Thor wipes his failure off his face when his hammer lands back in his hand, and he holds its massive form high. Lightning cracks through the sky, and thunder booms, rumbling the ground and shaking the monster's enormous form. Several more lightning bolts shoot from the sky to the hammer before charging back up then aiming for the beast. The lava monster jumps aside, and the lightning narrowly misses the giant's form and singes a black patch on the ground.

Twisting my palm around, I release my stored magic, trying to give the lava monster a jolt of pain on its hand. I cringe as the fingers curl, and the gap around us tightens. Instead of releasing us or opening its grip farther, the magic shock causes the hand to constrict rather than retract.

What just happened? Elan grunts, thankfully remaining still.

Grasping my next breath to answer is a struggle. "I just tried magic to get the monster to open its grip on us. It appears to have had an opposite effect."

Then maybe you should keep your magic to yourself, Elan gripes.

I grumble. "Sorry. But at least I tried."

Another crack grabs our attention as Thor holds Mjolnir high, lightning splitting the sky in all directions until it redirects and aims at the lava monster. The beast twists at the last split second, causing the lightning bolt to miss it again. I'm shocked that something so big can move so quickly. Either that, or it's just dumb luck.

Disappointment and frustration cloud Thor's face. He spins and releases his hammer, using Mjolnir's projection to fly his body straight at the monster's feet, knocking the beast to the ground. The jolt shoots through the whole body, including its hand, as its backside hits the ground. I wish all this jerking and jumping would cause the lava monster to release us, but my wish goes ungranted, and the hand doesn't release its grip, although it does loosen enough to give us a clearer view of our surroundings.

A view of Thor getting pummeled by the lava monster and knocked away shatters my hopes. That wasn't the image I was hoping for. His body flips and rolls before grinding to a halt. Almost immediately, the monster's empty hand swipes at Thor with claws extended, ripping a hole in his pants.

Through clenched teeth, I cry with dread. *That can't be good.* Scratches like that infected Elan, rendering her unconscious and almost killing her. Getting over that injury and the magic held within the lava monster's claw marks took a long time.

Despite the pain covering his face, Thor climbs to his feet and swings his hammer, releasing it at the lava monster before staggering awkwardly. Already, his actions seem more sluggish, and the lava monster has more time to move to one side, sending Mjolnir careening past unhindered.

A massive black fist swipes at the staggering Thor, pummeling him again and sending him flying several feet in the other direction with a final hit. Thor's body flops aside like a plush doll and thumps to the ground, unmoving.

I clasp at the crack in the fingers with both hands, trying to pry them farther apart. "No!" I scream, dread riding my voice.

Elan's tail twitches beneath my feet. *What is it?*

"Thor's been scratched by the monster. He's tried to continue fighting, but the scratch is already affecting him. He's being thrashed and thrown, and he won't get up." I stare at his unmoving body, willing him to move.

Elan gripes, *Well, that's it, then. We're doomed.*

"I know it's not looking good. But we can't give up."

Hmm. I disagree. The monster hasn't released us yet, so we're officially damned. She attempts to swivel, probably to see out of a crack.

"Stop moving, Elan. You're squashing me. If you keep it up, I'm not going to be able to breathe."

Sorry. I was attempting to help, but that's useless. I can't bite the stupid monster because it's squashing my face.

The vision of Thor's lifeless body is ripped away as the lava monster swivels. Vibrations rattle us, matching the walking giant's pace as the grasp on Elan and me tightens.

Chapter Two

My heart sinks—not only for myself and Elan but also for what happened to Thor. The last I saw, he was sprawled on the ground, unmoving. I hope he's all right. Asgard needs him, and he is also becoming one of my friends.

My body jerks with each giant footstep the monster takes, the reverberations traveling through its enormous body. The constant shaking rattles my bones, vibrating up to my neck and head and giving me a headache. For a moment, the movement stops, giving me a reprieve, which is shattered when the giant monster shoves its hand into a large bag and drops Elan and me into the center, swinging within the material.

The dark fabric completely blocks my view, especially when the monster seals the opening shut and swings the bag. The uncomfortable feeling of floating through the air comes to an abrupt halt when we slam into something hard and warm. The monster must have tossed us over its shoulder in the sack. My assumptions are confirmed as we sway roughly from side to side, swinging out then slamming into something solid again. My headache grows, along with additional bruises as I continually slam against the hard surface, sometimes unlucky enough to be squashed under Elan's form.

Elan grimaces. *Sorry. This is uncomfortable enough for me, but at least when you collide with me, your weight isn't unbearable.*

I groan, gritting my teeth, bracing myself as we swing out, and Elan's body pummels me again, squashing me against the monster's back. My vision seems blurry inside the dim enclosure, and I feel like I want to pass out. A slight depression creeps up on me. *Here I am, trapped again.* I was going to find out ways to learn more magic and make it stronger. Instead, I've been captured by a giant monster, and I can't do anything about it. My magic isn't big or strong enough to help protect me, Elan, or Thor.

My thoughts trail off to Thor again as sadness encloses my heart. I hope the monster didn't hit him too hard, and lethal magic hasn't filled its scratch, as with Elan's injuries. The sack enveloping us swings from side to side, and I wonder why this monster hasn't tried to kill me. I don't understand why it's carrying us.

Elan groans.

"What is it?"

This bag is made out of fabric, right?

"I believe so. Why?"

No matter how much I try, my talons won't cut it.

I roll my head back in defeat. "It must be tainted with magic."

Elan huffs, and hot air fills the sack. *That would be the only explanation. These talons have cut through many things stronger than a simple piece of fabric.*

The movement changes, and the swinging motion shortens for a while, turning my headache into motion sickness. I clamp my mouth shut, willing my rising stomach contents to settle. At least Elan isn't being slammed into me. Minutes seem to turn into hours as we swing smoothly from side to side. Unable to see anything to keep my mind occupied, my eyes droop with weariness, and my mind drifts into vagueness, eventually giving in to the pull of sleep.

Nightmares riddle every strand of a dream, carrying with them my concern over Thor and what happened to him, the future of Asgard, and what will become of Elan and me. Eventually, a peace takes over my dreams, only to be jerked away when a warm breeze brushes against my face. At first, I think Elan has expelled a hot breath over me until I open my eyes. Elan is facing the opposite direction, her scales glowing a deep orange-red. My eyes widen with fascination that quickly turns to dread as I scan our surroundings. The bag has fallen away, revealing a landscape made in my worst nightmare. I didn't know a place like that existed in the land of the living.

"Am I dead?" The words were a whisper tickling my circled lips.

Elan bends to look at me, her golden eyes glowing eerily with red. *Nope. This is definitely happening.*

Bile leaks into my mouth. A dark sky looms overhead, smothering ominous tall black mountains dripping with waterfalls of burning orange lava. Only the orange embers' glow illuminates the sky and surrounding land—arid, rocky ground, more mountainous than flat, with glowing orange rivers.

Residential structures are cut into the largest mountains in the distance, with lava waterfalls falling from all sides. A gust of hot breeze brushes my face, and I back up to Elan, pressing my body against her scales, taking comfort in their hard spikiness.

An eruption sounds not far away, and a blowhole

of lava shoots several feet high, firing out splotches of orange clumps. A golden membranous wing loops around me, and I press into Elan's side. Being a dragon, she would have some natural resistance to the heat and burning magma.

The surroundings have distracted me from the lava monster's swooping hand, and it gathers us up and plunges us deep into a hole. Then the hand opens, leaving us on the black rock floor. I don't know whether that is a blessing or a curse until I realize it's placing us in a cave, sheltering us from most of the exploding lava pits. A big gaping hole lines one side of the cave, giving us a view of a large lava river flowing directly from our doorstep.

Elan's protective wing wrapped around me furls as the large hand pulls out of the entrance at the top of the cave, exposing the glowing pits substituting for eyes as the monster peers down at us as though we are the size of small rodents.

This monster is enormous. I'm not surprised Thor had a hard time fighting it on his own. The glowing eyes pull away, and the ground rumbles underneath us at the tempo of its large footsteps.

My eyes remain wide as I survey our surroundings, my arms protectively crossing over my chest. "Where are we, Elan?"

I don't know. But from what I've heard, it looks a lot like Muspelheim, the land of the fire giants.

I approach the lava river and peer over the edge. "It's not Helheim? It looks like part of the underworld, a place fit only for the dead."

The scales above her eyes bunch into a frown. *I'm not sure. But wherever we are, it doesn't look friendly.*

Beads of sweat gather on my forehead and neck, and I yank at the long dark strands of my hair, tucking the wisps behind my ear. The ground shakes in even vibrations again, and I gaze up at the hole, shaped almost like a wide chimney, to see the glowing red eyes of the lava monster have returned.

A feeling of hopelessness swamps me as I gaze into the glowing red pits fixed on us, seemingly fascinated by the captives in its enclosure.

I mutter to Elan, "It's certainly diligent in watching us and making sure we can't leave. However, even if it wasn't watching, the only escape route is through that hole or past the lava river." Keeping my voice low and my eyes fixed on the lava monster's, I ask, "What do you think your chances are of flying past the peering lava monster?"

Sadness fills Elan's eyes. *I don't like my chances. The lava monster's hand nearly takes up the whole of the top of the cave. I could do it in an invisible form, but you don't have your cloak, so that kind of defeats the purpose. The monster is undoubtedly taking its job seriously.*

"I still don't understand why we're here."

Elan sits on her haunches then lowers onto her stomach. *Me either.*

Dizziness washes over me, and the arrows in my quiver rattle as I sit, leaning against Elan and taking comfort in the scales poking into my side. She rests her head on her front talons, and I gaze up at the hole only to find the disturbing red eyes constantly glowering down at us.

Frustrated by being watched continuously, I yell, "Why are we here?"

The lava monster remains unmoving, the unblinking eyes staring at us.

I ask again, "Why have you brought us here?"

Met with silence, I groan. "Where even is here? Where are we?" I glower when no answer is given.

After a few moments of silence, the lava monster straightens then turns, and the ground and cave shake as something large blocks the large hole above.

I cringe. "Please tell me it didn't just block the hole with its butt."

Elan cranes her neck, staring at the sealed opening, the scales above her eyes bunching together. Her mouth turns down at the corners. *It appears so. I just hope it doesn't have to go to the toilet anytime soon.*

I shudder. "That's so gross. However, I wouldn't be surprised if the only thing coming out of that is lava. Perhaps we should move to the side."

We do so, and I press against the hard, rocky wall. Within moments, the heat radiating from the rocks has become too much, and I pull away quickly, the arrows in my quiver rattling. Everything seems to have additional warmth in this land, like an internal heat that radiates to the surface, causing everything to burn.

Splashes sound from the lava river, and I retreat into a dark corner as some kind of monster wades through the scorching lava river, thumping its way past the cave entrance.

Chapter Three

The darkness enveloping me causes the hairs on my body to stand on end. The shadows bring with them an eerie sensation as I sink farther back into their embrace, watching the four-legged monster trudge through the lava. Hard dark plating similar to the lava monster's exterior resembles black rocks covering the creature's body. That layer looks like the scales of a dragon but lacks their beautiful colors and finesse. Whatever the thing is, it seems to hold off the molten river's searing heat, leaving the monster unaffected.

The lava bends like thick mud around the long legs of the creature as it trudges downstream through the river. The rigid plates around its mouth pull back, exposing a threatening display of teeth. It appears to be enjoying the river's scorching heat, trudging farther and swishing its head from side to side. Throwing its head back, it lets out a roar, opening a mouth filled with burning red magma. Long black spikes trail down its back, along the spine on an animal similar to a hound, except for the burning red eyes peering our direction. Its enormous legs trudge forward, its short tail dipping its tip in the melted river.

The creature sways our way, and my hands instinctively reach for my bow and nock an arrow. Gazing down the shaft, I wonder if it would do any damage at all if I hit the creature.

The doglike creature's tail finally passes the entrance, and I breathe out a sigh of relief. This whole realm, black and glowing with red, seems dangerous and uninviting. I long for the tall marble pillars and stony mountains of Asgard. Despite not being as green and welcoming as Midgard, they are still beautiful to me. Even the lack of Thor's playful taunting fills me with homesickness.

My gaze remains fixed to the last spot the four-legged monster was visible as I pack my bow and arrow away. "What do you think they want from us, Elan?" Briefly, I gaze up at the blocked hole, where the lava monster remains. "Why do you think they captured us?"

Elan steps away from the wall. *I have no idea. And if they were just after you, why did they capture me? Don't they think that I will put up a fight to protect you?*

I smirk. "Don't they think I'll put up a fight to protect *you?*"

She lowers her head to my height, and I grab her horn, tugging at it playfully.

Releasing her horn, I say, "Not that I think either of us has a chance of defending against these things alone. I'm only at the beginning of learning how to use my magic. It's not strong enough to use against these things."

Elan lies on her stomach, and I lean against her, leaving the quiver of rattling arrows on my back. I'm too afraid to take them off, in case we have to move in a hurry. After several uneventful minutes tick past, I rest my head against Elan's side and gaze up at the large backside—or whatever part of the lava monster that is—blocking the hole. The heat is wearing at me, making me sleepy even though my nerves are fully alert.

After a little while, the air pressure around us shifts as the monster moves from above us, revealing a part of the red-glowing sky. A puff of breeze drifts through the cave, and even though it was warm, the temperature drops slightly, bringing some relief from the trapped hot air and removing some of the stench of the heated minerals.

Elan cranes her neck, looking at the hole. *I wish I could see the stars. I miss them already.*

Expelling a sigh, I breathe. "Me too. What do you think the lava monster's doing?"

I don't know, but if that hole remains open, I think I'm going to try to fly out eventually. I'll wait and see. Hearing her voice inside my head brings me comfort, and my spirit soars over the thought of escape. Hiding my emotions takes an effort. The last thing we need is for the monster holding us captive to be able to read my body language.

Elan rests her head back on her front talons, her eyes trained on the hole. *The problem is I can't see if the lava monster is hanging around the outside or if it's gone.*

I pick lightly at the edge of one of the scales on her front leg. "That could be a problem."

We remain huddled together, and the ground beneath us vibrates slightly while rocks tumble from the sides of the cave above us. Our attention is pulled from the gloomy redness illuminating the hole to the cave, and Elan instantly shelters me with her wing. The ground and cave shake in rhythms different from the walking of the lava monster. The ache in my head is almost gone, only to be brought back with each vibration. My weapons rattle against my back, and the ground shakes so much that I have to stand to avert the pain in my bony backside.

With a question in my eyes, I gaze at Elan.

I have no idea. But the closer it seems to be and the

more it seems to vibrate, the more I think it's the pace of a giant's footsteps.

A shudder runs down my spine. "Great! Just what we need."

The shaking of the ground continues, and I pay attention to the tempo. Elan could be right. It could easily be the even pace of large giant footsteps, except these seem heavier, with a longer time between them than the footsteps of the frost giants we met in Jotunheim.

With wide eyes, I meet Elan's gaze. "How big would the giant be to make footsteps that far apart and that heavy?"

I don't know. Even in my head, Elan's voice is a hushed whisper. *I thought the lava giant was big enough. These footsteps seem heavier somehow.*

Larger rocks clatter off the cave interior and drop down, one narrowly missing my hand resting on a tall boulder. I yank it away and snuggle closer to Elan and the protection she offers with her wing. She wraps her wing around me, tucking me close to her hard scales. The heavier the footsteps become, the larger the rocks that topple from the cave's sides, some of them half the size of a human. I fret for Elan. Even with her tough scales, if they fell on her, they could still cause her harm.

As I peer out from under her wing, I spot a large

human-sized boulder toppling toward us, and I send out a bolt of magic, shattering it and sending slivers of black rock shooting in the opposite direction. I'm tempted to hold the rocks in place with magic, but I want to leave as much of my magic stores as possible ready for whatever is coming. Elan's wing tightens closer around me, squishing me against her body and tucking me slightly underneath her.

Unable to see much through the tiny crack she has left, I duck under her body and peer from under her forelegs. "I can't imagine something causing this much destruction to the ground is going to bring us good news."

We will take this as it comes. We have been through much together and will work out how to get through this.

I press against one of her large golden forelegs and inspect the hole above. The slow and steady footsteps approach until, eventually, something passes over. I brace myself, standing under Elan's huge form with my feet hip-width apart and hands balled into fists as the thing passes over. Something long and about the width of two of my arms curves in a seemingly never-ending loop. I haven't seen the beginning or the end. Eventually, it leads to something denser, blocking out the red glow in the sky. I squint, trying to work out what it is until one glowing red eye peers down at us, followed closely by another. The scrutinizing stare ties my stomach in knots. *Some pupils wouldn't go amiss on these creatures with lava-filled eye sockets.* The face alone tells me that this monster is even larger than the lava monster that left us here.

As an automatic response, I reach for the sword strapped under my quiver on my back. The scraping steel groans its protest, echoing through the cave as I yank it from its sheath and fling it upward. The metal gleams golden against the light of the lava, aiming straight for the hole, point first. With my magic, I guide the tip true to the target. At the same time, I grasp my bow and nock an arrow then send it directly at whatever is peering into this cave.

The thing moves, swatting my sword toward the burning lava river as though it was a fly. I call my sword with my magic, coaxing it to use its wings and return to me. I trust this will work as the arrow aims straight at the monster's eye. The monster swipes again, this time missing the target. The giant monster grumbles, and its eyes narrow as it pulls back, allowing the arrow to pass unhindered. A rumbling sound tumbles into the cave, resembling laughter drowned in lava.

Elan lowers her backside and braces her front legs as she roars the loudest and most impressive roar I've heard from her. It echoes up the cave and out of the tunnel. I wait, hoping this will have some effect on the monster. It does, but not the kind I was hoping for. The beast throws its head back, and explosive laughter thunders through the air.

Elan tilts her head to the side. *Dragon scales! What is this thing?*

"I have no idea." I wrap an arm around her front leg. "But clearly, it doesn't take us seriously."

Elan exposes her teeth in a silent snarl. *I know. How insulting!*

Despite myself, I can see the funny side and cackle briefly, receiving a glare from Elan. I shrug. "This thing is huge. How could it be threatened by something as small as us? It could swallow the two of us in one mouthful. Like we think we have a chance against this." I pull away the long dark strands of hair sticking to my sweaty neck. "It was quite pathetic of us."

My humor dissipates as the giant monster raises a sword engulfed in flames.

Chapter Four

Distracted by the flaming sword, I almost miss my sword's singing as the magical wings bring it back to me. A high-pitched whistle grabs my attention, and I catch it a split second before it collides with me. Clasping the hilt, I hold it across my front, poised and ready, even if the gesture is useless. I'm never giving up without a fight.

I set my jaw and fix determined eyes on the monstrous beast peering down at us.

Illuminated by the flaming sword, a malicious grin spreads across its face, and its glowing insides shine past a surprisingly broad array of sharp teeth. The head tilts to one side, and an eye narrows at us, having a closer look before pulling away. The added distance exposes the long, curving thing's identity as an enormous horn curling down the massive form to the waist. Several smaller horns, which resemble the impressive horns of a large goat, protrude from the head around the larger one. Exposed, impressively broad shoulders top a bare muscled chest and protruding pecs that would leave any warrior envious. I hoped this was a male, as the chest defined, and the largest of the creatures of this wretched realm.

The strange rumbling continues, growing louder when the creature opens his fiery mouth, and the sound explodes with laughter.

With a voice so deep that it sounds as though it has risen from the depths of the realm, he says, "Did you think that little sword and little arrow would do something to me?"

I scowl, and his grin spreads.

"Or did your dragon think that their roar would scare me off?" His laughter pauses as he observes us then throws his head back. "That's hilarious!"

The ground shakes violently, and I bend my knees to combat the rumbling and avoid more falling rocks. I imagine the only explanation for this destruction is that the monster has stomped his foot while laughing —the destruction growing as the laughter crescendos.

I almost feel insulted, Elan grumbles.

Crossing my arms and glaring up at the giant monster, I say softly into her ear, "I don't know about almost. I *am* insulted. Who does he think he is?

Although admittedly, he is a lot larger than us, so I guess he has a point."

More rocks scatter to the ground around me, and I dodge to the center of the cavern. Unwilling to let them hit my head, Elan towers over me, her protectiveness rewarding her with several stones falling on her body. Her lips pull back, baring her broad array of sharp teeth at the monster.

Annoyed by his continued taunting, I call up to him, "What do you want with us?"

His cackling halts, and I continue, making the most of the silence. "I can't imagine dragging a Valkyrie and her dragon here is your normal entertainment." Huffing, I pull my arms into a tighter cross.

The ground stops shaking, and he peers down at us, a curious expression crossing his hardened grotesque face, resembling both man and monster. "You are not here for my entertainment, mark my words. I wouldn't go through so much trouble to grab you or bring you here."

Not staring at his lava pit of a maw is hard. Every time he opens his mouth to speak, a fiery red burns within, making it hard to concentrate. Still, I control my emotions and splay my legs. "Then why did you bring us here?"

The giant monster straightens his back, showing us his full height with the added distance through the hole, and tucks his chin. The cave entrance frames his face and some of his body, exposing more of his bare muscled abdomen. "Do you not know who I am?"

"No. Why would I? I have hardly even heard of this place. That's assuming we're in Helheim." I lift an eyebrow. "Is that where we are?"

His monstrous hairless brows lower. "No. You're in Muspelheim."

I fail to hide the shock on my face.

"Don't they teach you about this realm in Asgard?" he asks.

"We were taught very little about Muspelheim at the Valkyrie academy. It isn't a place we would normally go. As you probably know, our main focus is on Midgard."

His hairless eyebrow arches, and he waves his sword. "Ah, yes. So you can reap the souls of the brave warriors for Valhalla."

Keeping a straight face takes all my strength. I didn't know that was common knowledge.

He grins. "Don't worry. It isn't a secret. I know Midgard is the place you go because you are after the poor warriors' souls, enslaving them to Valhalla for eternity."

I stare at him. "I wouldn't say that exactly. How do you know so much about what we do?"

The huge male clasps his stomach, his fingers rippling over his six-pack, and lifts his chin as he bends backward, roaring his laughter to the sky. "Your naivete is rather amusing." He chuckles until it mellows into amused huffs. "I can't believe you know so little about me and my realm."

I grunt, unamused that he is finding me so comical and angry at feeling foolish. My thoughts turn toward the Valkyrie academy. We should've learned more about the realms other than Midgard and Asgard. I've learned more about the different realms since serving under Thor than I did during my years at the academy.

Elan's voice interrupts my thoughts. *Don't beat yourself up. He's baiting you. Valkyries aren't meant to be fighting in every realm. They're meant only for only one purpose. You must remember your role changed when you were chosen to be Thor's representative. It's a higher purpose than merely reaping souls for Valhalla.*

"Reaping souls is an important role for Asgard," I argue.

Exactly! You should be proud of that, not ashamed because you don't know everything about other realms.

I pull my gaze from the giant mocking me to Elan, finding her golden eyes gleaming down at me with compassion and pride. Yet again, I'm thankful that this dragon and her mother have chosen to represent me and support my struggles. Because of them, I have turned my services into something more powerful than simply getting wingless Valkyries recognized for being more than just slaves.

"Did I ever mention how much I appreciate your support and friendship, Elan? I thank my lucky stars every single day that you entered my life."

Her head tilts to the side, and a funny little smirk spread across her face. *No. You haven't actually said that.* She lifts a scaly eyebrow. *But I know, and the feeling is mutual.* She quickly shoves me with her nose, affection in her golden eyes.

Despite our situation, I smile. "All those things wouldn't have been achievable if I didn't have the support of you and your family and if they hadn't convinced the other dragons. Even if we don't make it through this, I'm extremely thankful that I lived my short life with you in it."

Her brows push together. *Hey. We can get through this.* She flicks her nose briefly at the giant monster, still staring down at us. *This has got to be another idiot giant with the brain capacity of a nut. I hear they are quite dumb. You must've seen that on Jotunheim.*

Pushing my lips to one side, I stare up at him. "I

don't know, Elan. This one seems to have a few more brains than the frost giants."

Large red eyes zoom in at us as they peer into the hole. "What are you two talking about?" His head tilts, and he seals the hole briefly with one eye as he gets a closer look at us. "Are you planning to escape?" His voice reeks of amusement. "If you do, you will be unsuccessful." He straightens, pulling his face farther away and giving us another a full view of his monstrosity. "Although it would make life rather interesting, you could at least let me introduce myself before you plot to leave. I am Surt, the leader of Muspelheim and the fire giants."

I frown. "I thought this was part of Helheim and under the leadership of Hel."

"Is that what they're telling you these days?" He taunts me again with his amusement. "How little you know about Muspelheim."

"Then educate us!" I snap. "Didn't Hel send one of your lava monsters to Asgard to attack us as a warning?"

Surt snorts, and fragments of molten lava fall to the ground around us, but not before Elan covers me with her fireproof body, protecting me from the burning debris. I think the snort was supposed to be laughter, but I wasn't sure. When the burning embers stop falling, I peer past Elan's wing at him.

His massive lava-filled mouth turns up at the corners in what I guess is a smile. "Oh, how you are wrong. As if I'd send my pet to Asgard for Hel's bidding. For a start, she would have to give me something in return. In order to do that, she would have to speak to me." He rubs his upper arm. "Except for rare occasions, she speaks to no one but the dead." He shrugs. "I'm too alive for her to be bothered with me."

My brow crinkles into a frown. I find it hard to believe that anything that burns internally with lava could be alive. I push this thought aside. That's a consideration for another day. "But a lava monster attacked Asgard," I protest.

Surt shakes his massive head, the long, curved horns swiping at a few floating embers. "No. The lava monster was not attacking Asgard. The lava monster was there to get you."

Chapter Five

"What?" I stare at him in confusion. "But that was a little while ago. Why would you send a lava monster to get us?"

"No. I sent my minion to get *you*." Surt's mouth settles into a straight line.

I set my fists on my hips. "So you sent it to attack me?"

"No. You're not listening." Annoyance creases the gap between Surt's fiery eyes. "I sent it to collect you."

"Then why did it attack Elan?"

"Because your dragon is always with you, and I'm guessing she went into defense mode and attacked first."

"It nearly killed her," I growl.

Surt's massive shoulders rise in a shrug. "What can I say? It was defending itself."

The answer doesn't sit right with me, but I didn't

see what unfolded when I was within the tunnel's confines. Although I knew my heart was always going to believe Elan.

He must have read the disbelief on my face. "My pet turned up to collect you. It would have sensed you and followed you. Except your dragon blocked the tunnel you disappeared into, and she attacked it. My pet, or what you call a lava monster, was attacked by your dragon. It was only retaliating and trying to get rid of your dragon so it could get to you."

I cross my arms over my chest. "That's a rather extravagant way to try to collect me. I don't understand how you would even know that when you weren't there."

His lava-filled smile sends a chill down my spine. "I have my ways."

"How?" Raising an eyebrow, I press the point. "How could you possibly know what happened?"

"Let's just say I have friends in places, and I received a message."

Moving out from under Elan's protection, I uncross my arms. "I still don't understand why you'd be bothered to get me. If you're after Thor, he was there trying to stop this monster from getting me. He was protecting me, and the monster could have grabbed him instead."

Surt chuckles. "I'm not after Thor."

I flail my arms out to the sides. "I can think of no other reason why you would want me here."

Surt gazes at Elan. "Despite that you've befriended the dragons and turned them into friends, for not only yourself but also all the other Valkyries and the gods and Asgard."

I need all my might to clamp my mouth shut and stop my jaw from dropping. *Has the result of my small personal quest spread through the nine realms?* "Well, yes. I don't see how that is your business."

He huffs, and light embers shoot out of his nose and float on the air. "That is mostly true. It doesn't involve me. But the reason I've grabbed you is that, for many years, I've been looking for a mate."

Despite my situation, I laugh, shaking my head. "Your mate is certainly not going to be me."

"You." He scowls with disapproval. "No. It's not you. You are too violent and aggressive. You aren't the most beautiful maiden that I have seen."

I lay on the sarcasm. "Gee, thanks. I still don't get why you would want to grab me."

"It's because you have access to the most beautiful maiden in the world." His gaze turns dreamy as he focuses on the lava-lit sky.

My mind swirls, trying to figure out who he is thinking about. Unable to come to any conclusions, I say, "You'll have to help me out. The only maidens I know are Valkyries—and some goddesses, but I have little to do with them."

He leans over the gap above the cave, his burning lava eyes narrowing on me again. "And that is where you are lying."

"What?" I bellow in outrage. "I'm not lying!"

"Hmmm!" He sounds unconvinced. "I have it on good authority that you know who I am talking about and you have access to her."

As though sensing a threat, Elan steps protectively over me, ready to block me from anything he may send my way. I rest a hand on the scales on her chest, a silent thank you before stepping out from under her protection. With nothing to hide, I face him directly. "I honestly don't know who you are talking about. I have contact with hardly any other females, and the goddesses don't pay me any attention."

"And that is where you are wrong." His voice thunders down the hole, and his brows crowd angrily over his burning eyes.

With one swift movement, Elan wraps her wings around me, leaving only my face exposed, giving me room to assess the situation.

Something hits the side of the cave, and rocks drop into the cave, narrowly missing us. "I know you have access to Freya." A threat stains Surt's voice. "I want her to be my wife, and I can never find her. But one day, she will be my wife."

The sides of the cave shake again as more rocks drop around us. I wriggle under Elan's protection to free my arms and blast the falling stones away with my magic.

With an open-mouthed gaze, I find my voice faltering. Pushing past the blockage takes a few moments, but I say, "I don't know why you think I'd know her. As far as I know, she doesn't even live on Asgard."

In truth, I spent time with Freya a couple of years ago. Despite being the goddess who rules over the Valkyries' natural enemies, the angels of death, she helped me protect Asgard. She instructed our known enemies to fight for Asgard's safety against the dark elves' invasion and Loki's army of wild dragons with dwarf giant riders. From my brief encounter with Freya, I learned she is sensual and thrives on love and understanding, the opposite of the fiery abnormality standing in front of me, the leader of the fire giants. He doesn't deserve Freya's affection, and I could never see her giving it to him. Furthermore, because she has been kind to us and helped against the attack on Asgard, I could never give up her location even if I did know where it was—which I don't.

Since my association with Freya isn't a secret on

Asgard, as it's known that I called her for help, I tell him part of the truth. "I don't know where she is. I haven't seen her for at least two years. As far as I understand, her residence is shrouded in secrecy."

He clasps the entrance of the cave with both hands and glowers down at me. "But I have it on good authority that you have been to her residence."

I gulp. Somehow, he has gathered information on me and my movements. "She did have me taken to her location. But I still don't know where that is. I was blindfolded and kept from knowing the location of her camp." And now that I hear this giant demanding her location, I understand the reason behind that secrecy.

More rocks crash around us as his grip of the cave tightens. Elan and I dodge the falling debris until the chaos stills. I stand on a large boulder that landed near me. If he keeps this up, the level of the rocks will lift us closer to him. A growl rumbles down through the entrance, whose shape accentuates the volume, and I clench my teeth, cringing.

His gaze is threatening. "I do not believe you are telling the truth. Would you like to start again?"

"I am telling the truth. I haven't seen her since that time a couple of years ago. I don't know where she is or where she stays."

After another crash, more rocks rumble into the

cave, and I miss deflecting one that rebounds and crashes onto Elan's side. She flinches as it tumbles over the canopy of her extended wings, attempting to protect me, and I flinch as it falls to the ground.

Another loud grumble reverberates through the cave. "I know you know more than you're letting on. You must come clean with me. The sooner you do this, the sooner I'll let you out without harming you… and your dragon," he adds at the last second. "But if you don't come clean with me, this promise is void. I will leave you in here, stewing over the consequences of your silence. You cannot leave this realm without my help or the help of my pets."

My silence only seems to aggravate him more. He pushes off the cave and stomps off, the ground rumbling with each step.

Chapter Six

Setting my jaw, I gaze at the last spot I saw Surt. I don't like our situation, but I couldn't give up Freya's location even if I knew. The canopy of Elan's golden wing retracts from over me, accompanied by a wince, pulling my attention back to my friend. The offending rock lies only a few feet away. It's huge.

Rounding her large form, I try to peer at the spot the boulder hit on her back. "Are you okay, Elan?"

She attempts to cover a small grunt that escapes her when she moves to face me. *Yes. A little bruised, but not too bad.*

"You didn't have the saddle to protect your back." Regret nibbled at me even though it was an honest oversight, considering I didn't know we were about to be kidnapped by a lava monster. "I left it next to my apartment after I took it off Sobek, I mean Loki." I growl at my error.

Elan nudges me with her snout. *I'll be fine. It's just a bruise. My scales protect a lot of that, remember?*

"I know. But it still would've hurt. I heard the impact, and it was a huge boulder." I continue to assess her scales. "Any broken bones?"

Kara! Stop fussing. We have to get out of here. Remember, that's the most important thing to focus on. I'm guessing you're not going to tell him where Freya is. She lowers her head, leveling her gaze at me. *Not that I want you to.*

"No. I'm definitely not going to tell him where Freya is. But it's true: I don't know where she is. Even if I did, I wouldn't tell him. She deserves much better than him, no matter what he threatens us with. Besides, I don't give up friends who help Asgard or me."

Elan scoffs. *She can definitely do better than him. That wouldn't be hard!*

Burning with annoyance, I glare up at the hole of the cave. "What is it with the gods thinking they can take any goddess as their wife? So old-fashioned."

Yeah, just like they think they can own all the dragons and control them and make them agree to unfair alliances, Elan says with spite.

"We worked on their attitudes and treatment of the dragons and ended up with a fair outcome. Don't you think?"

Of course. I was just using it as a reference to their selfishness.

"Indeed. Maybe we can work on changing their view on goddesses and thinking they can own them."

Sounds good. Then maybe we can stop them viewing Valkyries as only battle maidens who aren't supposed to get married and settle down and have children. Or if they do have children, it can only be with particular warriors to create more Valkyries.

I huff a laugh. "I don't think it's quite that bad, but close. That view is very old-fashioned as well. Thankfully, they haven't tried to pawn me off to create Valkyrie babies."

They probably think you have a few more good battle years in you before they start using you for breeding.

"I'm not going to do it." I kick a rock, and it clatters across the ground. "There's no way they can pair me off with someone."

Elan tilts her head to one side. *I can see this will be another battle you're going to have to face and try to overcome.*

I glare at her.

Hey! She retreats and straightens her back. *It's not my fault. I completely agree with you. It's another thing we'll work on with the gods and the head Valkyries.*

My chest heaves with a massive sigh. "I know. It's

not something I want to think about. Thanks for bringing it up." I roll my eyes.

Rocks clatter to the side, knocked by Elan's talons as she paces the cave, her gaze traveling to the hole above and the opening toward the lava river. *What do you think? Should I try to fly out of here?*

Happy for the change of subject, I join her and assess the openings available. "I would say our only chance would be past the river," I muse.

Rumbling sounds from above, and the hole above is blocked again, I assume by the backside of the lava monster.

I huff in disgust. "Are we looking at the lava monster's butt again?"

I think so. If it is, it certainly has a strange but effective way of blocking the hole. Although I think it forgets that I have wings.

Something moves over the entrance opening to the river of lava, and disappointment crumples Elan's facial scales when solid black legs dangle past it. The legs don't block the entire entrance yet remain a deterrent and a promise of a warning.

"I guess that's our answer. It hasn't forgotten you have wings. I'd say it thinks it can catch you on your way out." My heart sinks at the thought. "I wouldn't know which direction to go anyway. From what I can see, the land is covered in black rock and flowing lava, giving very few distinctive landmarks, and I certainly can't see the Yggdrasil."

The world tree must be here somewhere. Maybe it looks different down here. It's supposed to touch all nine realms. Elan sits on her haunches. *And I assume the giant brought us down here through the Yggdrasil.*

Anger churns deep within as I stare at the hanging legs that swing once as though reminding us of their presence. I stoop down and pick up one of the many fallen rocks, one that fits perfectly in my hand. I toss it then catch it in the same hand, glaring at the obstacle threatening our freedom before being overcome by temptation. I peg it at one of the dangling legs. A loud clank reverberates through the cave as it collides with the back of the lava monster's calf. The leg flicks forward for a few seconds before swinging back over the opening menacingly.

The walls of the cave rumble as the legs slowly swing wide and more rocks crumble from the inside lining, falling around us. Glowing pits resembling eyes peer over the edge of the river opening at us, the red flashing in a warning that it's still watching us, waiting for us to try to escape.

Instantly, Elan shifts in front of me to block any threat from the monster. Her wings drape around me, leaving me to peer out from behind her front legs. The lack of pupils makes it impossible to tell who the eyes are looking at or if they can see me.

"I guess that answers our question," I say softly.

Elan's protective stance remains unwavering until the monster finally pulls away, taking its fiery red glare with it. The draping legs kick out and swing back into position, partially blocking the entrance to the river. Rocks clatter around us again, and I push them away with my magic, smashing them against the cave walls.

With the threatening pits gone, Elan says, *We're just going to have to wait for our chance. It's not going to be impossible, just tricky. That strange thing works like a dog watching over that hole.*

"Maybe it has more brains than we give it credit for."

Elan spreads her wings and shrugs. *Who knows? I wouldn't be surprised if it can sniff us out like a dog on the hunt.*

Chapter Seven

In the dull light cast by the lava river, I collect the arrows scattered over the ground, dislodged when we were unceremoniously dumped in this cave. Only a few had managed to remain tucked in my quiver, ready to grasp when needed. At first, I was surprised that my weapons weren't confiscated, but my wonderment at remaining armed was abolished when I threw my sword and shot the arrow at Surt and he found my efforts laughable, incapable of injuring or harming him. Thanks to his reaction, I hadn't bothered collecting the weapons earlier.

With the talk of escape, a new hope infuses my veins, and I set my mind to gathering my things in preparation. Clasping my sword hilt over my shoulder, I lift it, listening to the metal sing before releasing it with the satisfaction of its accessibility.

Casting one last look around the cave, I'm satisfied that I've retrieved all lost weapons, and I slump down against Elan. Heat radiates through her scales —a warmth I don't need, yet I lean in, resting against her and soaking in her friendship and comfort. It's a welcome relief from this depressing place.

Elan curls into a ball, wrapping her head close to my body, almost in a protective enclosure. Her golden eyes glimmer in the orange glow of the lava river, her face thoughtful. The river's golden light is mesmerizing as my mind swirls with ideas and plots to free us from this entrapment. The warmth from the lava glazes my eyes, and my body thrives in the short rest as I think things through.

I tuck a hand under one of Elan's scales, touching the soft flesh underneath. The simple gesture brings so much comfort. I can even feel her body relaxing into my touch. The connection wipes away some of the stress of being kidnapped and taken to a foreign and dangerous realm.

Elan must be exhausted. She just recovered from the lava monster's first attack, only to be kidnapped, her body thrown into another explosion of stress.

Hot breath shoots out of Elan's nostrils, and she rests her head on her front feet. *Let me know if you come up with any ideas on how to get out of here. My guess is that these mind games aren't going to go away, and our only escape is planning a dash past the legs of the lava monster.*

"Something tells me that you're right, Elan. Although we can both use a little bit of rest to try to recoup energy."

Elan's eyelids close slowly before being jerked open. *Ain't that the truth.*

I wrap an arm around Elan's front leg. "I wish we had our friends here, Valkyries and dragons. We might have more of a chance. The reality is that Thor may still be unconscious, and no one will know where we are. They may not even know that we're missing."

She twists her head to land her sad eyes on me. *I hate to say it, but with the condition Thor was in when we were taken, I don't think anybody will know we're gone. I doubt anyone else saw the lava monster leaving.*

Defeat and disappointment creep into my optimism, taking over my muscles, which go lax, and I flop against Elan, her sharp scales digging into my flesh. I ignore the discomfort, taking solace in knowing my scaly friend remains by my side. "You're probably right."

I assess our surroundings, taking in every inch, and study the access points again to assess if I've overlooked a loophole that will get us out of here. I can't tell when Surt will be coming back, and when he does, if I don't give him the answer he seeks, we may need an escape route, however dire it is.

Minutes, if not hours, tick by, bringing the discomforting feeling of being lost. If not for Elan, I would be very lonely. I've studied every part of the cave, only to come up empty-handed for brilliant ideas, and my gaze returns to the lava lake, my eyes drooping with exhaustion as the warmth lures me to sleep.

A strange scratching pulls my focus upward, and I search for the source. The glow of the lava bathes everything in an orange-red light, making it hard to spot the source of the noise.

The scratching continues, and I squint, focusing within the darkness, higher than the light of the lava. But I fail to catch any movement pointing to the cause of the sound. Looming darkness, thick enough to cut, prevails in the top half of the cave, the hole remaining blocked by the lava monster.

The scratching continues, setting my nerves on edge. Worried that it might be a dangerous creature exclusive to Muspelheim, I continue searching the shadows cast by the orange light behind the jolting rocks. Eventually, something glowing a deeper orange darts across the far side of the cave. I blink. The object is hard to discern in the light from the molten lava river. Perhaps the fire embers are reflecting against something, but then it seems to glow a different kind of red. Whatever it is, it continues to move in a circular downward motion, heading toward us.

Pushing off Elan, I stand to get a clearer view of the approaching creature. My fingers tingle with anticipation, and I gather my magic while unhooking my bow and nocking an arrow to aim at whatever is scurrying along the wall.

In a place like Muspelheim, it could be anything. As Surt pointed out, I've been uneducated about this realm and the creatures it holds, other than my personal experience with the lava monster. Whatever this is, it could be just as dangerous but in a small form.

Elan shifts behind me, and her presence looms over me protectively even though my arrow remains nocked and ready to release, aimed at the anticipated location of the moving creature. As though oblivious to the threat we present, the animal continues to scamper, and its scurrying echoes as it circles around and down, crawling closer to our position.

My eyes narrow, focused entirely on this thing. It maneuvers to a rocky ledge and pauses, standing upright and exposing a furry white chest that burns with the lava river's golden glow. I squint harder. *It can't be,* I think.

"Elan, are you seeing what I'm seeing?"

Do you mean Ratatoskr? She sounds almost bored. *I*

told you Yggdrasil must come to Muspelheim somewhere even if we can't see anything that resembles a tree. He is renowned for carrying messages to every part of the realm.

I gawk at the little thing, my eyes widening as I realize the truth. Elan is right. This is that tiny, annoying rodent. He has followed me even to the depths of the fire giants' realm.

Beady little black eyes focus in my direction, peering over the sharply pointed nose. The high-pitched voice reaches my ears as he crosses his arms and leans against the rock wall. "There you are. I finally found you." He scurries down a couple more levels. "My source was right. The talk on the rumor mill is that you've been taken to Muspelheim."

My eyes narrow at the little rodent. "How could you possibly know that?"

The squirrel waves a paw at me. "You'd be surprised by the connections I have." He looks me up and down. "Clearly, this time, it was right."

He scurries farther down the cave, weaving over the jutting rock surfaces.

For a moment, my heart skips before beating rapidly, and a glimmer of hope rises to the surface as I stare at the squirrel coming my way. "Are you here to help us?"

The squirrel halts midclimb, momentarily freezing before leaping onto the next flat surface and facing me. "Are you serious?" His face is awash with disbelief. "What do you possibly think I could do in a place like this?" He spreads his arms wide and swings them wildly, indicating the blocked hole and the lava river's opening.

The erratic beat of my heart slows as I realize that was a stupid thought. The idea of this annoying, sarcastic squirrel helping us doesn't make sense. Besides his apparent lack of care for others, he's too small. He couldn't do anything against the fire giants.

I roll my eyes and lean on one hip and attempt to be insulting. "My mistake. A self-centered little creature like you wouldn't want to help anyone anyway."

Ratatoskr puffs out his chest, the white fur almost beaming with orange from the lava glow, illuminating his pride. "You got that right. Unless there's something in it for me, I'm not going to do a single thing to help you."

I scrunch up my nose with distaste. "I should've known better."

He nods, and his self-righteousness is hard to miss, coupled with a demeaning tone. "Yeah. You should have."

Glowering, I wish the sulfurous fumes from the lava river would render this little rodent unconscious. "Then what are you here for, little rodent?"

The squirrel poses his head and plasters a smirk on his face while circling a little paw around his temple. "You are a little nuts. I knew there was nothing held up here." He rotates his claw some more. "I seriously would've thought you would know better by now. This isn't the first time I've seen you."

"Right. Of course." I drag the last few words out. "You're here to bring me a message."

He shakes his head in disbelief. "Thank the Vanir! She's finally got an answer right."

Chapter Eight

At this moment, I can't conjure the words to describe how irate I am over this little rodent. Only moments before, I'd been longing to see a familiar face that could reconnect me with Asgard. A few short moments spent with this little critter had shattered that hope. Now, all I want to do is push his little face out of my sight.

"So, what insulting message have you brought me?" I ask, leering at him.

Ratatoskr chuckles through his teeth, his breath sucking in and out in short stints of rugged hissing. "Oh, this is a good one. I've been looking forward to delivering this one."

I shove my hands onto my hips. "Then why don't you just tell me? And then you can run on your merry little way."

Elan shifts, reminding me of her presence looming over me, attempting to protect me from harm. Even though Ratatoskr is tiny, his insults have the potential to cause more damage than something physical. My heart warms, knowing that she's here for me, no matter what. I stroke her front leg, taking pleasure in the roughness of her scales under my fingertips.

The beady eyes narrow on me. "I have a message from Odin."

My teeth clamp together, and dread travels through me. I can't help thinking of the last time I saw him sitting in his room, bedridden and weak. He still hadn't recovered from the terrible vision he had at Mimir's well.

Pulling me from my thoughts, Ratatoskr continues, "Although I don't think this is a message I would usually carry." He polishes his claws on his furry white chest. "As you know, I only bring messages with insults. I have a feeling this one carries more truth than an insult." He shrugs. "But I thought I'd bring it anyway because... I do love it!" He stretches his front paws up in the air as though he's worshipping the top of the cave.

I frown at the squirrel's excitement and focus on my concern. "Is Odin okay? Is he feeling better?"

The squirrel chuckles into his paw—his sharp teeth obscured by the tiny claws. His beady eyes torture me with their amusement, and I glower and cross my arms. When Ratatoskr is finished chuckling, he pulls his hand away and stands straight, one eyebrow cocked. "You could say that."

When he doesn't elaborate on his statement straightaway, I press him. "What do you mean?"

"As you know, Thor was injured, and he's in the healer's care. Hearing the news was enough to bring Odin out of bed to check on his son as soon as he could. Before he decided to leave his room, he was granted some final news."

When he doesn't continue, I coax him by saying, "And?" while rolling my hand as an indicator to hurry the story up.

Ratatoskr chuckles briefly into his paw again, eventually pulling it away and standing straight. "And he heard that you released Loki." The rodent's words were sharp and precise, and his mischief-filled eyes never leave me as he waits for my reaction.

A gush of air expels from my lungs, and my shoulders cave. Shame sends my gaze to the ground. "I didn't..." I stammer. "I didn't technically release him. In truth, he escaped from under my guard." I hate myself for looking at him, almost pleading for understanding, as if I could get that from this rodent.

Ratatoskr clucks his tongue. "Oh. Don't worry. Odin's been told that. But..." He shrugs. "It didn't make any difference." The smirk on his face wipes away my fleeting plea for understanding. "You should've seen how deep red his face turned. It could've matched my fur, if not that lava out there." He tosses his head backward. "And the steam coming out of his ears! Phew! I could've sworn he was a dragon." The rodent drags out his words, his tone mocking and emphasizing the severity of the actions.

I cringe, dread running down my spine, and grit my teeth. "And what was his message?" I want to cover my ears and not listen although that would achieve nothing. I have to hear what Odin had to say. I can't do anything to change my actions. I can only face the music and get it over with. Maybe he'll help Elan and me to get out of Muspelheim if I listen.

Ratatoskr stands straight, clasping his claws behind his back and puffing out his chest. "Your message from Odin is…" He sucks in a breath and clears his throat. "You are the most useless Valkyrie he has ever seen. He should have left you and your kind as slaves. He wished he didn't allow you into his mind and heart, giving you access to change the way he deals with your kind. The Valkyries without wings are an abomination and shouldn't be rewarded by serving him and reaping warriors for Valhalla."

"What?" My jaw drops as I gape, analyzing whether this was an insult or the truth. I have to agree with Ratatoskr's earlier statement. It's too close to the truth and how things used to be to think this is just an insulting message carried by Ratatoskr to get my attention.

Ratatoskr holds up a paw, his back remaining rigidly straight. "Don't yell at me. Remember—"

"You're just the messenger," I finish in a cynical tone.

He drops his paw, and amusement dances through his beady black eyes. "Yes. You're finally learning." He adds in a condescending tone, "Bravo."

Clenching my jaw, I ask, "Is that it?"

"No. There's more. That was just a small insult."

"A *small* insult?"

"Yes. I could think of more to add, but that wouldn't be Odin's words."

I can almost feel steam coming out of my ears. "Then get on with it!" I snap.

"Because of your serious mishap of letting Loki free and not catching him again even though you spent over a day with him—"

I interrupt, flailing my arms out to the sides. "That's not fair. He was in the form of Sobek, Elan's brother."

Ratatoskr raises a claw at me and shakes it. "I'm not finished. And I am not the judge and jury. I'm just passing on a message."

I roll my eyes and let impatience seep through my voice. "Then stop wasting time!"

"With pleasure." Ratatoskr puffs out his chest as though preparing for a long speech. "He said that because you let Loki out and didn't recapture him when you spent a full day with him"—he holds up a claw at me again as a warning not to interrupt—"that he now forbids you from entering Asgard. From this moment on, you are hereby banished until you have retrieved the deceitful Loki and have him secured within the mighty Odin's grasp." He lifts his chin and looks down at me. "There. I finally passed on the message."

I hate that I can't hide the hurt on my face from this conniving rodent. "What about all the good things I've done?" My bottom lip quivers. "I've done so much good for Asgard. I'm going to rectify this situation, at least eventually. But I can't do it if I'm stuck here. I don't understand. How am I ever going to get out if he isn't sending me help and is banishing me instead?"

Ratatoskr shrugs nonchalantly. "No idea. That is for you to work out. Goodbye." He scurries up the cave wall, heading toward the top, where the lava monster still blocks the entrance.

My mouth is agape as I stare up at him. "But—"

raitor! Elan grumbles, sitting on her haunches.

The rodent scurries up the side of the cave, the glow of the lava river on his red coat unmistakable now that I know what to look for. My heart thumps rapidly in my chest as my brain attempts to process the unpleasant outcome and information dumped on me. I can't believe I've been banished. After a moment, I pull my thoughts together and realize that we're still stuck in the middle of Muspelheim with no one to help us escape this sweltering enclosure. As much as I don't enjoy Ratatoskr's company, my only lifeline and potential help is running toward the top of the cave.

Even though he's out of reach, I extend my arm, reaching for the faraway rodent as though I could stop him. "Wait!"

Ratatoskr pauses on a rock, his glare evident even

from a distance. "What is it now? You always do this —call me back every time I'm disappearing."

"Well, if you didn't disappear so quickly, I wouldn't have to call you back," I retort.

"I'm a busy messenger!"

"Can you please come down lower so we can discuss something?"

"I have nothing to discuss." His gaze becomes pointed with annoyance.

I roll my eyes. "The discussion is about a message I want to send."

"You know I don't discuss things," he repeats through his teeth.

"Okay. Okay. Then I want to pass on a message. Just come down and give me a moment."

He groans loudly before dramatically turning and slowly climbing back down the wall of the cave.

As I watch him, my mind swells with insults I could send to Odin. With regret, I push them away though expressing them is tempting. After all, I'm already banished and too far away to hear his punishment. By the time I see him again, his anger would probably have subsided. Humming, I marvel over the different things rattling through my head. Tempting though they are, I hope to re-enter Asgard someday, and to make that happen sooner, sending insults is probably not the best choice at this point.

The scratching claws grow louder as the squirrel closes the distance, his red form zigzagging down the rocky ledge.

Crossing my arms, I lean against Elan. "Just wondering… Have you seen Loki lately?"

Ratatoskr reaches the lowest ledge and stands straight with his paws on his hips. "What makes you think I would have seen Loki lately?"

"Oh, I don't know." I wave a hand dismissively. "Perhaps it's because you were giggling with him when he was in dragon form in Jotunheim. You could easily have informed me that he was Loki and saved me all this hassle. My friends and I could have plotted to recapture him as soon as we arrived in Asgard."

Ratatoskr tilts his head to one side. "Don't you start with me. I gave you plenty of hints that it was Loki. If you're not smart enough to put it together, it's not my fault." He shakes a claw at me. "I am not responsible for your stupidity." He blows at the bottom of the feet. "Hurry up with the insult. These rocks are rather hot, and it's hurting my paws. What insult do you want me to give to Thor"—he raises a furry eyebrow—"or Odin?"

Shaking my head, I chuckle. "Oh, I am not sending an insult to Odin. You really do think I'm stupid if that's what you think I mean to do."

Ratatoskr presses his furry backside against a wall, taking turns standing on different feet. "Okay then, who are you sending an insulting message to?"

"To Thor."

Ratatoskr straightens. "That could take a while. He's still out cold."

My heart crashes to my stomach. "What?" I wipe the sweat off my brow, my skin cold and clammy despite the heat. My mind swirls with dizziness as I try to think of other options, but I fear I'm clean out. Perhaps I could send a message to my friends. I shake my head at the thought. They might not understand it because they don't know Ratatoskr very well and might take the mock insult as reality.

"I need to get a message to someone, letting them know where I am. It's clear you're not going to tell someone I need help, out of the goodness of your heart."

"Pfft! Sweetie, I don't have a heart." He sits on a rock ledge, letting his fur take the brunt of the heat, and lifts his feet. "Fire away! I can hold the message for Thor until he wakes up. I can't guarantee I'll call in on him every day, though."

I take a deep breath and let it out with a hiss, knowing Thor is probably my only hope. "Okay. Tell Thor it's kind of him to have a little nap and let that lava monster take Elan and me. He could have stopped it. Instead, big, tough Thor, with his lightning and hammer, decided to play a little sleeping game and let the lava monster take us to Muspelheim. Now I'm stuck here, in this heated hole, kidnapped by Surt. Thanks very much, Thor."

Ratatoskr cackles. "I love it! You're getting a little better at this." He points a claw at me and winks his approval. "I'll be glad to pass that on when he finally wakes up. Who knows when that will be." With a pleased expression, he gazes at me. "Now, is there any other message you need me to carry? Or are you finished with your messages?"

I nod. "I've finished. But can you please get the message to Thor as soon as possible? I don't know what Surt's plan is for us down here. We could be in a lot of danger. He seems to think that I know where Freya is, and I don't."

"Hmm. Is that so?" His pointy face scrutinizes me. "I thought you had visited her and called to her for the war on Asgard."

"Well, yeah. But that was so long ago, and I don't know where she resides."

"Oh?" he says, sounding unconvinced. "All right. That's it now." He scurries up the side of the cave to the hole, disappearing after the lava monster releases him.

I'm surprised at the ease with which the cheeky

little rodent can travel through the realms, unhindered even by monsters. Eyes fixed on the hole, Elan drops to her stomach, and I slump next to her, wriggling in close and leaning against her scales. My eyes remain fixed on the blocked hole where Ratatoskr disappeared, amazed how something so small could be the most annoying personality I've dealt with.

My gaze drops to the opening to the lava river. The monster's legs remain dangling over the top.

"Are we ever getting out of here, Elan?" I clasp the edge of one of her body scales and fiddle with the pointy edges. "The one person I think can save us is wiped out unconscious, thanks to the lava monster."

She circles her neck around me, resting her head on her talons, not far from my leg. *Don't worry. We'll get out of this soon one way or another. Rest up. You need your strength.*

Stretching my legs in front of me, I attempt to relax, only to have my feet twitch, restless from the fear and doubt churning through my thoughts. I've just been exiled from Asgard. Telling me to rest up is easier said than done. Also, we could do with some help. I don't want to be stuck here and want to get my life back to normal. I need to help Thor protect Asgard from the potential threat of the three siblings, especially after we recapture Loki.

At the thought, my forehead creases, and I mutter, "If the children are only going to attack Asgard if Loki is captured, wouldn't it be better to leave him free?"

Elan hums. *Possibly, but then that would probably leave you homeless for the rest of your existence. Not only that, we don't know what Loki's true intentions are.*

I fold my arms over my stomach and pull my knees to my chest. "You're right. At times, he seems to be working for Asgard, and other times, he seems to be working against."

I shake my head, pushing aside my doubts. My first focus should be getting out of here… after some much-needed rest. Visions of Odin being proud of me again as I hand Loki over fill my head, despite my attempt to clear my mind of all worries. Time passes slowly until my eyelids eventually droop and my head tilts to one side. Pulling my knees in closer to my chest, I snuggle into Elan. The hard scales bring me comfort as they press into my skin, for I know she is near, and I'm not alone. I wriggle, resting my face against her front leg just in front of her chest, and listen to her breathing. The slow and monotonous sound sends me off into a deep, calm sleep, finally pushing the day nightmares away.

Something jerks me awake. I jump as a rock

crashes on the ground, not far from our side. Springing to my feet, I glance up at the top of the cave in time to see a massive hand sweep into the hole, aiming directly for us.

Chapter Ten

The enormous hand lowers, swiping one direction then the next and pushing us back into a corner. The arm shifts as the body attached to it moves to a better position. Something lowers over the top of the opening to the lava river, fixing my attention on a glowing red eye peering over the top. One long, curved horn sweeps down into the molten river and out again, forming almost a full circle.

Elan lurches protectively in front of me, her legs sprawled and her lips pulled back into a snarl, blocking the burning eye's view of me. Undeterred by Elan's efforts, the hand whips across the cave, swiping the large golden dragon out of the way.

Helplessness overcomes me as her large form is flung to the side like a small toy, slamming her against the wall.

A yelp reverberates through the cave, coupled with the thud of the impact.

Yanking my eyes from the mesmerizing lava gaze, I check to see if Elan is okay. A worried frown creases my forehead as I wait for her to move. I attempt to go to her only to have my effort wasted as a hand sweeps over, clasping me around the waist and yanking me upward. Struggling to push my hands down, I squirm but fail to shimmy out of its grasp. The grip is too tight, and no matter what I do, I cannot loosen its force.

My breathing grows ragged as panic weaves its ugliness through me.

I peer over the side of the hand to see Elan climbing to her feet, staring up at me. She looks tiny down there.

The hand yanks me through the hole, away from her concerned gaze. I catch a final glimpse of her golden eyes staring up at me as another hand swiftly blocks the hole enough to prevent Elan from flying out to help me.

I'm lifted farther until I'm dangling in front of a large dark face, eyes burning with lava and two horns that would impress the strongest of goats, shadowed by several smaller horns. The large horns are so big that they appear to be almost useless—ornaments, mainly used for show—whereas the smaller ones surrounding them seem a more practical size and an actual threat.

With wide eyes, I hold my breath as I let my gaze travel up to look at the hideous face now level with my body. Surt's form is enormous, and I flinch when I realize I'm being held in a direct line with the giant's mouth.

Lifting my focus to Surt's eyes takes all my effort. I don't want to be this close to pits filled with lava that act like eyes. I think they focus on me, but that's hard to tell when the eyes have no pupils. They seem more like lava abysses, never-ending gateways to a fiery death I don't want to experience.

The fingers shift, and one clasps me around my waist. I attempt to wriggle out of it but can't, eventually giving up and steeling my fear as I gaze up into the glowing eyes, mesmerized by the lava pits.

The enormous mouth spreads into something like a smile, exposing not teeth but red molten rock. That makes sense—Surt would have no need for teeth when anything consumed can be incinerated. I don't know how this giant can talk. I don't want to be this close to Surt.

"So. You've had long enough to think it over?" His voice is deep, with an edge that expresses how difficult it is to talk through melted stone.

"To think over what?" I ask, playing dumb.

Impatience shows on his hard face as fiery evil

climbs into his voice. "Are you going to tell me where I can find Freya?"

My insides recoil, and I want to curl up into a ball. This giant is huge. After a moment, I pull my thoughts together, reminding myself of what I stand for and why I'm protecting the goddess. I shove away the fear and encase my spine with emotional steel to bring strength back into my shoulders. "I don't know where Freya is. I've told you this." I lift my chin, knowing that's not a lie. "I don't know how you think threatening me is going to make me suddenly come up with something I don't know."

A deep rumble, low and menacing, sounds in his throat. "I have it on good authority that you know where she is."

I cross my arms and tilt my head to the side. "And who tells you I know?"

His eyebrows push into a vee as annoyance washes over his face. "I have it on good authority from Loki. He tells me that you know. He sent me a message through Ratatoskr."

"Then he's misinformed."

Surt shakes his head. "I believe him, not you."

"Hmm. Interesting. Do you know Loki personally? If you do, you should know that he's mischievous. Don't you think he could be misleading you to distract you from something? Please tell me that you have at least considered this. You cannot trust what he says!"

Surt nods his head, expressing a noise of agreement. "I know he's a weasel, but on this, I'm inclined to believe him." He lifts me to eye level. "I don't trust what comes out of your mouth."

"Do you think I'm going to change my story because you're threatening me?" I flail my arms out to the sides. "Why don't you capture and question him like you're questioning me? See what he tells you then."

A strange emotion flickers across his features then is washed away by anger. "Tell me or else."

"Or else what? Are you not listening to me?"

His hand shifts around me, and somehow those massive fingers clasp onto my quiver still attached to my back. He shakes me lightly, my dangling legs and arms whipping in different directions. I drop my gaze downward, thinking maybe I can abandon my quiver and drop to the ground. The idea is quickly shoved away when I see the distance to the ground. As much as I've wished for it all my life, I can't fly. Before I know it, I'm dangling over an open lava pit. Surt has reclined his head and raised me, dangling me over his horrid mouth.

Shivers rock my body as I gaze down into the

fiery pit. Knowing it's a mouth seems to make it a lot worse than just a bubbling pool of molten rock.

His hand pauses, the heat from his mouth warming my boots to the point that my feet feel like they're on fire. I retract my legs, pulling my knees to my chest, and hug my arms around them. Nothing I do is going to save me.

My weight pulling against the quiver forces the straps to dig into my underarms and shoulders. Large beads of sweat form on my arms and forehead, but I'm too scared to move to wipe them away. With one wrong move, I would be Surt's meal, for sure.

The muscles in my arms, abdomen, and legs ache from the pressure of holding them curled against my body. I don't know how long I've been dangling here —probably only a few minutes— yet hours seem to have ticked away. Every little movement of the fire giant's hand sends bolts of fear straight into my stomach. If his fingers open or I slip, I will cannonball right into that lava pit.

Eventually, he moves me away, holding me out to look at me again. "Now… are you going to tell me where she is?"

Releasing my legs, I let them dangle awkwardly below, the straps from my quiver cutting into my underarms and causing them to go numb from the lack of circulation. I stare Surt straight in his burning eyes. Maintaining a steely expression is hard, with fear raising the bile in my throat. "As I said, I don't know where she is."

"But you do know how to call her."

I huff. "I don't know where you get this information from. Sure, I admit, she came once before when I called her. I was lucky. Somehow, I managed to do it, and she came to us during a battle to help save Asgard. I haven't found anything to use to call her since then, and if I did, she probably wouldn't come."

"Why would you say that?"

"She's a goddess!" I exclaim. "She probably won't remember who I am, and if she did, I doubt she would be listening for my call. I've had contact with her for only a couple of hours in the past, and she helped only because she had a hunch that another army was brewing trouble. She requested we stay in contact so we could sort out that battle. The battle is over, and without that threat, we no longer need to keep in contact."

His facial expression doesn't change.

I groan. "When are you going to believe me?"

In my frustration, I shoot magic at his nose. It screws up, appearing almost like rock folding upon rock. The reaction is minor, but it gives me enough incentive to shoot more magic at probably the most tender part of his body. He shakes his head, trying to rid himself of the discomfort and giving me hope that this may be working. Maybe my minute amount of magic is doing something.

I consistently send magic bolts at his face and cry, "Put me down!"

Frustration explodes through my body as he ignores me, yet at the same time, it gives me power to increase my magical intensity. I'm happy that my magic works, and I know I've stirred up some reaction, at least. The energy seeps from my body, leaving each magic attack weaker than the last, and my arms grow sluggish, causing the throws to become sloppy. I fire my last few bolts of magic until his nose wrinkles and he shakes his head.

His head folds back then shoots forward, releasing an enormous sneeze. Hot scalding breath blasts me, loosing me from his tentative grasp on my quiver. My terror rises, matching my speed as I shoot backward, straight toward the river of lava.

- Chapter Eleven -

I scream, my body a projectile through Muspelheim's sulfurous air. Nothing is there to protect me or stop my fall. Surt's massive hand swipes for me—concern flashing briefly over his face. He narrowly misses, leaving my body careening toward a scorching death. I scream again, flailing my arms and wishing I had wings. I know that's a useless wish.

This must be it. This is going to be my end—after everything I've struggled for.

Surt swipes a dismissive hand at me. He's given up trying to save me even if I am the only one he believes can call Freya.

Then my back slams into something, and I'm yanked upward, away from the glowing river. Twisting, I search for whatever changed my direction. The straps of my quiver dig into my underarms, rubbing a deeper chafe along the front of the shoulders.

That's a pain I'll gladly put up with, happy to watch the lava river shrink from underneath me as I rise.

The arrows rattle in my quiver as my legs dangle beneath me while I'm dragged through the air. I search again for the thing grasping me, thinking that maybe the lava monster caught me to help Surt.

The air above me is empty. Nothing is pulling on my quiver, saving me from falling to my death.

Shutting my eyes, I thank the nonexistent rescuer and suck in deep breaths, calming my nerves and clearing my other senses. I rise in patches to an almost monotonous beat, and I realize with each rise, I'm hearing the flapping of wings.

"Elan! Thank you." I breathe the words, keeping my voice soft, not sure how good Surt's or the lava monster's hearing is.

Of course I'm going to catch you! I'm not going to let you fall to a fiery death. Her voice was most welcome in my head. *I've been floating around invisibly since Surt grabbed you. It's easy now that I don't have to worry about you giving us away.*

My flight continues to rise and dip in time with the flapping of her wings, and I welcome the hot breeze pressing against my face. For these few moments, everything is beautiful, almost perfect. Elan's just rescued me from certain death. Even better, I am safe in the grasp of a friend.

Elan flies across the lava river, leaving dark rocky piles underneath us. Searching the land, I find everything in this realm appears to be made of dark rocks or molten lava. The land is desolate—barren and threatening—the red and black heightening the arid land's nastiness. Nothing nice exists in this place.

Gazing over my shoulder, I spot Surt diminishing in the distance, which gives me some hope. The lava river lies between our captors and us. "Come, let's get out of here. I hate this place!"

Carrying you like this is getting rather tiresome. Do you think you can put up with what I did the first time you rode me?

I trudge through the depths of my memory, trying to remember everything we did on that first flight, in the early days. Unable to pinpoint what she means, I say, "You're asking a lot, expecting me to remember. That was ages ago."

Oh well. If you don't recollect, then you're just going to have to deal with it. Brace yourself! Suddenly, she throws me.

As I hang in the air, waiting and hoping her invisible talons will catch me soon, my stomach lurches. My legs and arms sprawl as I drop, flipping and facing the ground, attempting unsuccessfully to glide like a bat as the land below rushes up to greet me. Watching history repeat itself, I'm struck with the memory of the time I fell off the edge of a cliff and she clasped me, tossed me, and caught me on her back. That was the beginning of my very first ride.

With a thud, I collide with what must be her back. Well-practiced, I hook my hands onto her invisible scales and scramble into a sitting position and wrap my legs around her neck.

I purse my lips to one side and push my sarcasm to the front. "Hmm. Thanks for the adrenalizing jump to my memory. I remember now."

Despite my situation, I can't help but smile as her brief laughter fills my mind. *I'm glad I could jog your memory.*

She swerves, missing a smaller mountain. Even without her saddle on, the feel of her massive form underneath me brings me a feeling of security. It's a step closer to getting out of here. Surveying the horizon, I find nothing friendly and certainly no sign of a way out of this realm.

Where to? she asks. *I don't know which direction to go.*

"Me neither. I can't see the Yggdrasil anywhere or anything that would resemble the World Tree."

I peer backward. Surt and his lava monster are lagging, a distance that is closing quickly with every enormous step they take. A sudden wish overcomes me, that I had grabbed my dragon-scale cloak before visiting Elan. If I had it, we could both be invisible. Instead, I'm exposed to the elements and the prying eyes of the fire giants and their monsters.

The warm air brushes against my sweaty skin, cooling me despite its heat. I can almost smell the freedom from Surt's grasp. First, though, we need to find a way out of this horrible realm. With each flap of Elan's wings, my excitement grows, along with my hope.

Movement underneath us catches my eye.

"What's that?"

Dread fills me. The ground appears to be growing. Deep lava pits rise, along with the rock around them, giving the burning holes the appearance of eyes. More rock pries away from the ground underneath us, forming into another creature.

Elan tilts slightly to get a better view of the progress below, her tone suddenly panicked. *That's another lava monster, and it's growing out of the ground.* She swoops upward, twisting, narrowly missing a limb clasping at me from the other direction.

Flinging to one side, I dig my hands between her scales and clasp them with white knuckles. I need all my strength to not fall off. Gritting my teeth, I peer over my shoulder, catching sight of one large hand of this new lava monster, swinging our direction. Its digits hook as it tries to swipe at me and catch us both together.

The lava monsters must be smart enough to know that Elan is invisible below me. At least this time, the claws are retracted, not ready to scrape down Elan's side and embed the magic that severely injured Elan last time, almost killing her.

We are battered from the other side, and Elan flings us in the opposite direction. I glance back and spot the second raised hand of the lava monster. I cling tighter to Elan's scales, the sharp edges biting my flesh. She weaves and swerves, attempting to right herself while heading toward the snaking lava river.

Surt and his minions remain behind us. Each step they take lodges more tension in my spine. I shake it out and return my gaze forward. We narrowly managed to escape the last lava monster's grasp, and before they get any closer, we need to find a way out of here. Despite the lava monster rising from the ground, if we fly higher, we may miss spotting our exit.

Endless stretches of menacing mountains with lavafalls splay before us. Nowhere I look holds any hint of a way out of this realm or shows any of the greenery of the Yggdrasil.

I worry my bottom lip. I'm out of clues.

Elan flies over the lava river. *I don't like things growing out of the land. I'm going to follow the river. Any monster from this land should be highlighted by the glowing molten stone. Keep your eyes open.*

She rocks from side to side, swerving with the curves of the river. We cover a great deal of land, yet every time I glance over my shoulder, Surt and his two minions seem to be catching up.

An explosion bursts from the lava river several yards ahead, and flames shoot into the sky. I shriek, almost letting go of Elan's scales. She veers upward harshly, attempting to avoid the molten geyser. But as I eye the spot the explosion took place, my mouth drops open. The glow rises higher, pushed by the river rising.

I shriek. "What's going on with that river?"

I don't know, but it's something weird.

My eyebrows push together into a frown. The lava appears to be growing out of the river. Right before my eyes, it gathers and forms a shape.

"No way! That can't be!"

Elan doesn't answer, but I can feel her shock reverberate through my mind. The lava in the river is diminishing, reshaping from a flowing river into something else. Two large horns form on the top of a head, a snout growing long under black holes for eyes. When the snout finishes extending, it tapers off under two nostrils and opens, exposing a vast array of pointed teeth. The lava moves around the shape as though the skin is alive with it. The forming creature stretches higher, growing a long neck with spiky scales down its long neck, leading to fiery wings outstretched. It grows within a few seconds, a presence ten times larger than Elan, towering over us. The creature isn't fully formed, yet it's clear what this is.

Fiery dragon scales! It's a lava dragon. I thought they were a myth.

"Clearly not." My spine stiffens in shock.

Fire shoots at us from the dragon's mouth, and Elan dodges to one side. The body emerges farther out of the remaining lava in the river, only a small puddle underneath. Detecting where we are heading, it flicks its tail with the rapidity of a striking snake and wallops Elan on her side, just behind my leg. The heat from the lava seeps through my leather pants. I'm amazed how it knows exactly where to hit Elan, for she's still invisible. The creatures of this realm must be smarter than they look, unless this dragon and the lava monster can sense her invisible form.

Elan yelps as the impact sends her flying to the left with such speed that she doesn't have a chance to regain control. She smashes sideways against a mountain, crushing my leg between the rocks and her scales—my leg throbs with pain from the impact. She flips as we fall, pushing off the side with her talons.

We project into the air, only to be swiped by the lava dragon's front feet. It hits us with the fleshy part in the middle rather than the talons—the impact sends us careening again toward the mountainside.

I grit my teeth as we fly toward the rock wall, and I attempt to scamper away from the impact while still hanging on. The impact is hard as we slam into the mountainside again. This time, I swear I hear the cracking of bones.

Pain screams through my body, almost drowning out Elan's groan in my head. Limply, she slides down the mountain toward the ground.

The dragon made of lava roars, the sound deafening. I cry out in pain as rocks slide across my leg, ripping into my leather uniform. We reach the bottom with a thud, and I slam to the ground and tumble off Elan as she turns visible.

This is not a good sign. She must be unconscious or hurt badly and unable to keep up the ruse. Elan lies unmoving in front of me, and overcome with dread and pain, I slump on the ground momentarily. When I attempt to rise to my feet, the pressure on my left ankle is agonizing, and I cry out in pain. It doesn't feel right. I clamp my teeth and struggle to stand on my right leg. Each hop in Elan's direction jars through my body, sending the vibration through my left leg. Between each hop, I gasp with ragged breaths but continue, determined to reach Elan's side. Seeing her like this brings back recent nightmarish memories, and my heart shatters.

"Elan." My voice breaks. "Elan, are you okay?"

She doesn't answer. My leg pain grows stronger, and I take a brief rest and feel down the injured leg. My hand brushes something hard, and after further investigation, I realize my thigh bone is sticking through the skin. I retch to one side, my stomach swirling with unpleasantness. It takes all my effort to still the cyclone of nerves in my stomach and concentrate on Elan.

A dull orange light shines down, and hot breath blows from above. I gaze up to see the dragon made from lava peering over us, its mouth open in a half grin. Its nostrils flare as it takes in our scent.

I wave a dismissive hand at it. "Go away! You've caused enough damage."

It keeps looming over the top, its black eyes focused on us, watching us as though it's on guard.

The ground vibrates in an even rhythm, and I ignore it, positive one of the lava monsters is stomping over the land. Pushing aside my pain, I stagger up to Elan's nose and tap it with an open palm, trying to awaken her. When this doesn't work, I shake it slightly.

"Elan. Elan, are you okay?" Urgency grows in my voice with each passing second. *Not again. I don't need her to be injured again or worse.* I push the thought of worse options out of my mind, not allowing myself to think along that path.

Shoving my hand against the soft part of her nose, I inject healing power into her. As no lava creatures' claws have struck her, I hope this will help her mend. I repeat this several times, hoping for a result before the ground-shaking monster comes close. Even when I know the beast is leaning over me, I don't stop. I continue injecting the healing power until I'm ripped off the ground by an enormous hand, and pain blasts through my body from the movement of my leg. The ground shrinks beneath me as Elan's eerily still body accompanies me.

- Chapter Twelve -

Wrapped in the massive hand, we're carried for many ground-stomping paces. The large hand opens, revealing the inside of the same cave and crushing my spirit. We thought we had escaped. We tried, yet here we are, back where we started—trapped inside the cave guarded by the lava monster with no way out. Making it worse, we are now injured. My body screams when we're tossed onto the ground with a thud. Pain soars from my broken leg up to my hip and straight down to my foot. I crush my eyes shut and hiss through my teeth.

The ground beneath me shakes violently at an even tempo. Small rocks break loose as I can only imagine Surt stomping away, surly after we nearly escaped. Eventually, the vibrations fade, and I wrestle with the agony shooting through my body from the shakeup. When I get a hold on my pain, I pry my eyes open only to find Elan's motionless body slumped next to me, which fills me with stress. The rough treatment didn't even wake her.

"Elan! Are you with me?"

Her beautiful golden-scaled body doesn't move, and I struggle to keep my hopes up. I need to get to her, but first, I need to pay a little attention to my own condition. I'm no use to her injured. Being a Valkyrie, I have fast healing powers, but the next part isn't going to be pleasant. I have to do something about this leg.

Rolling up and sitting is a considerable effort. When that round of pain subsides, I grit my teeth and gather the courage to feel down my injured leg again. My hand grazes the broken bone protruding from the skin, and I cry with pain. Amazingly, my leather pants are still mostly intact over the fracture. The lump from the bone is evident through the fabric, with only the smallest hole where a bone fragment sticks through. I grimace. This is going to hurt.

My breath catches as I run my hand over the hole again, feeling the sharpness of the protruding bone. Somehow, I have to get this leg straightened so it can heal. I need something to grasp the other end, and Elan is out cold. At least, I hope that's all that is wrong with her. I shove the negative thought out of my brain and focus.

A dark shadow passes over the cave, drawing my

attention. I'm confident that I'm looking at a part of the lava monster blocking the hole again.

After clenching my teeth, I scream up to it, "Hey, you! I need your help."

The shadow remains fixed over the hole.

"Lava monster. Or whatever you call yourself. I need your help."

It takes a moment, but the monster starts to move, and the shadow pulls away from the hole, replacing it with the lava-filled pits that act as eyes, peering down at me.

"What do you want?" Its voice is obscured just as before, as if it's drowning in lava.

"My leg's broken. I need you to hold my foot so I can straighten it."

The lava-pit eyes narrow. "I'm not helping you. You are a prisoner."

"I get that, but you want information, don't you? Or at least Surt does." I pause, trying to read the monster's expression, then continue, "I can't think, I'm in so much pain like this. Perhaps if you help me straighten my leg to help the healing process, I'll be able to focus more and give you the answers you need."

I'm not sure if my bluffing will work. Unlike the frost giants, this giant has remained silent as it guarded us. Without much interaction, I'm not sure how intelligent it is.

The glowing eyes stare down at me for a while longer, sending shivers down my spine. Eventually, it huffs, filling the cave with breath hotter than the air already in here. "I guess you might be telling the truth. I will hold your foot." The enormous hand weaves through the hole, and the glowing eyes peer down over the edge of the lava-river opening, staring into the cave.

"What do you need me to do?" His voice sounds more gargled, probably from the different position.

"If you can hold my foot steady, that would be good."

He braces my foot between his forefinger and thumb. The squeeze of his fingers on my foot is uncomfortable but is nothing compared to the pain of the broken leg.

Briefly, I inject some magic to clamp the blood from flowing freely through the open wound. "Hang on tight and don't let go." I clamp my teeth together, knowing this will be excruciating, and brace my hands on the warm ground after wiping my sweaty palms on the leather at my waist. "Okay."

With a rapid push of my arms, I fling my body backward, ripping the protruding bone back into my skin and slamming the broken ends together in a straight line. My vision goes black, and my head spins as the pain drags me into unconsciousness.

SWEAT TRICKLES over one closed eyelid, welling in the cavity. The numbness blocking my thoughts is slowly edged away by rough stones sticking into my side. Slowly, I pry an eye open, my eyelid fighting against the invasion of the salty sweat as I attempt to focus on the cave dimly lit by the orange lava glow. I don't know how long I was out for, but the stiffness in my body tells me a while has passed.

When my brain starts to piece things together, I pull myself up into a sitting position, careful not to move my leg, the action accompanied by the clatter of my remaining arrows in my quiver.

Gently, I press my fingers over my thigh, feeling for the result of my backyard medical practice. The hole in my skin is mending. From what I can feel of the bone through my thin thigh, the straightening has been successful. Tenderness still surrounds the area, yet it seemed to be subsiding thanks to my Valkyrie healing abilities. It appears to have gone well.

In the dim light, I assess the amount of blood pooled around the leg. The collection is small and coated in a thin crust because of the length of time. A small smile of pleasure crosses my face. The magic to stem the blood flow worked well.

Even though the wound and bone are healing well, I look for something to secure the bone and keep it straight. Being on the safe side is best, in case it hasn't mended enough to handle a little pressure. Finally, I settle on my sword and yank it from its sheath between my back and quiver. I use the tip to cut two strips off my leather uniform around my waist then strap the sword against my thigh. It's an awkward fit, with the blade being too long against my thigh, yet that is needed to stop the bones from moving. My Valkyrie healing ability shouldn't take long to mend it enough that the splint will no longer be needed.

With my leg secure, I push with my arms and slide on my backside across the warm stones toward my beautiful dragon friend. Elan's unmoving form dampens my mild pleasure from my healing and fills me with panic.

I scramble to her front, holding my hand before her nostrils and praying for hot breath to cover them. Within moments, warm breath streams out of her nose as she exhales then reverses as it's sucked back in, weaving over my fingers.

"Good. You're alive. Now, I need to see what's

wrong." I stroke the end of her nose, hoping my touch will awaken something in her.

Since I know she's breathing, I focus on other parts of her body. Her legs are folded awkwardly underneath her, alerting my suspicion that they may be damaged.

Sliding on my backside, I make my way over to the exposed legs, assessing them and feeling for broken bones. They seem to be intact. I maneuver to her far side, pulling on her scales to help me rise to my feet. Grabbing the top wing, I stretch it out, checking the bones and membranes. When I don't find anything untoward, I fold it back by her side. I shuffle around her, using mostly my good leg and skipping lightly on my healing leg.

Blood has gathered around her, and her bottom wing lies in a strange position, partially underneath her body. It looks like she needs help healing, or she won't be able to fly.

I set to work on the small bones in the exposed part of the wing. I straighten the first bone, hold it in place, then allow the healing magic to flow out of my palms and into the damaged area. Each bone mended raises a small smile on my face. Slowly, I work my way around her body, healing any open wounds along with the bones. I don't know where the larger puddle of blood stems from. I hope it is a collection from every injury, not something more sinister hiding underneath her massive form. Just in case, I press more healing magic into her through the soft skin under her scales, coaxing it to slow down any blood loss, buying time for me to get to the wound.

Although healing the small wounds brings me comfort, I know from the position of her wing that her larger bones have a more substantial break. The problem is that I have no way to roll her onto her other side. Her form is too big to budge in any direction, and nobody could drag the broken wing from underneath her massive form without causing it more harm. The yanking might break the wing further or tear a hole in her membrane. Even if I were at my full strength, that would be an impossible task.

With every visible wound healed, I continue injecting healing energy into her through her soft nose until my knees go weak and raising my arms becomes an effort. My energy depleted, I crumple to the ground, draping over a large rock close to Elan's massive form, and rest my head on my folded arms. My eyes remain open, fixed on my recuperating friend's condition, taking in her body, thankful she's still alive. My eyelids droop, and I force them open. Remaining awake is a struggle as I cling to hope that she'll wake up soon to keep me company in this dreadful place.

Chapter Thirteen

Jolting awake, I curse myself for falling asleep again. I'm torn between the needs to stay alert and to grab the sleep I need to function. The time we've spent in this fiery realm is undecipherable. Without the sun's rise and the company of the moon, each day or hour blends into the next. The lava-filled fields under the dark sky look the same no matter how many hours have ticked by. One thing is certain: I've spent way too long without a decent night's sleep.

Prying my cheek off the rock, it twinges where a point dug into the flesh. I massage the spot lightly with my fist, stimulating the circulation, before pushing off the stone to rest on one hip. My bones ache with each movement after sleeping in such an uncomfortable position. As I straighten, I study Elan. My concerns dampen slightly with each movement she makes. Her restless stirrings are welcome, giving me hope for her recovery. A clunk sounds as I shift from my hip onto my backside, which drags my attention down to my leg. I forgot about my broken thigh bone until my sword sheath clanked against the rock.

I run my hands along the length of my thigh and stop when I reach the hole in my leather pants. The tenderness is gone, even when I poke the area softly. I finish by running my hand down the leg, concentrating on the bone. Thanks to my Valkyrie blood, the wound is mending rapidly. At the rate it's progressing, I'll be able to remove my sword splint shortly.

My stomach groans with hunger. Not knowing how long I've been down here also means I don't know how long it's been since I ate. A buffet at the palace sounds delicious right now. I'm so hungry I think I could eat the whole display.

That thought is quickly tainted when I remember I'm no longer welcome at the palace. And it doesn't stop there—I'm no longer welcome in Asgard. I rub my crinkled forehead, trying to wipe away the worry and pain of being banished. Thanks to Odin and his unforgiving ways, I'm no longer welcome. I made a grave mistake, but I thought he would've shown me some leniency after everything I've done for Asgard. After all, I kept his little emotional breakdown a secret from everyone. As usual, our relationship has seemed to go one way ninety percent of the time.

Hoping to prove myself once again, I drag my soul out of the depths of mourning the loss of Asgard and focus on Elan again. Slowly, I shift to one knee with my splinted leg straight behind me. Using the rock, I push myself to standing and shuffle toward Elan, placing most of my weight on my good right leg while skipping lightly on the left, and a pleasant surprise fills me. As I step with my injured leg, the pressure doesn't hurt as much as I feared. In fact, I feel barely a tingle of pain. Just in case the bone hasn't adequately fused, I keep the weight on my left leg to a minimum, not wanting to disturb the healing process. My healed leg will bring us the best chance at survival.

My progress is clunky and unrefined, but I don't care. No one is going to see me. All I care about is the golden dragon in front of me.

I drag myself to her nose, where I reach around her snout and rest my forehead on its surface. Touching underneath one of her scales, I feel for the soft flesh and search her face.

Her eyes open slightly, and my heart skips with joy.

"You're awake. That's great!"

She moves slightly and groans aloud. *Barely!* Her

hot breath bathes me, adding to the existing heat of the cave. Groggily, she says, *My head hurts. If it weren't for the rest of my body feeling just as bad, I would think someone drugged me.*

"That's understandable. You were knocked unconscious, and your wing was broken. I've mended some of it, but it needs more mending."

Slowly, Elan rolls onto her stomach and off the broken wing, which causes her to groan with pain and bare her teeth. She looks ready to bite someone's head off. Then her jaw clamps as she struggles to hang on to sanity while forcing down her agony.

That hurts so much! she groans.

Despite myself, I smile slightly with empathy. "That's understandable. I broke my leg too."

You did? I had no idea. She turns her head sharply, her lips covering her gritted teeth while she stares at me, her eyes pausing on the makeshift splint of my sword sheath. *Is it bad?* Despite her own pain, her eyes fill with sympathy.

Stroking the soft part of her nose, I attempt to ease her worry. "It was. The bone stuck through the skin and protruded slightly through my leather pants. With the lava monster's help, I managed to get it straightened." I whistle and shake my head. "Now, that was painful! I passed out."

Elan's lips pucker with distress. *That sounds*

nasty! Her eyes travel over my full leg, stopping at the hole, which exposes a small amount of skin. *I can't see it now.*

I shrug. "You know how fast Valkyries heal. It was a while ago now, and I've already mostly healed. I'm just keeping this splint on and not putting my full weight on the leg to make sure I don't hinder the healing process." I note the pain still in her eyes. "At the moment, I'm more worried about getting you better. Let me look at that wing."

As she straightens taller, allowing me full view of the other side of her body and the broken wing, I shuffle around to her injured side. Each time she groans, I cringe, sympathizing with her pain. Now that I have access to her full wing, I line up the broken bones and heal each one individually. I'm thankful that the Valkyrie academy healer, Anita, spent the time to teach me to do some healing. That wasn't a talent that Gilroma, my magic teacher, had spent time working on.

I set to work on the breaks in the largest bone, holding my hands over the injuries and willing them to heal by my magic, which saps my energy with each fracture. I use the bubbling lava river as a reminder to keep going, pulling more strength from determination until it becomes too much, and I take a small break. The more I heal, the more frequent my rests become, and each successive time, my energy takes longer to recover.

In my weakened state, my stomach growls in protest. I need food to refuel my body. Surt hasn't sent any nourishment to quench my dry throat or still my roiling stomach.

After another round of healing, I collapse to the ground beside Elan. "We need to get out of here," I whisper, watching for any movement at the hole the lava monster is covering.

You don't need me to tell me.

My eyes droop with weariness, and I rub my cheeks, trying to stimulate the circulation in my face and head. "Most of your wounds are healed. I have one last spot to check and inject with healing magic."

She circles me with her head, stretching her neck to gaze down at me, her eyes intense. *What is it?* The echo of her voice in my head gives me some oomph.

"I'm not sure. I can't stay here much longer. I haven't given away anything yet. But the way things are going, we need to find a way to get out of here before I become careless or Surt becomes desperate. I don't want to be responsible for any more bad things happening." I rest my head back against Elan's golden scales, taking comfort in their hardness. "I know Thor's not going to come for us. He's probably still unconscious, or Ratatoskr hasn't checked in on him to give him the message."

Now, that wouldn't surprise me, with that little rodent. I'm starting to think he's worse than Loki.

I look up at her. "You may be right."

Levering myself up again, I set to work on the last of her injuries then check the wounds I've already worked on. Seeing her condition improving lifts my spirits slightly and helps my strength return more quickly, but my exhaustion reflects in Elan's eyes. Healing takes a lot of energy.

"First, we're going to wait for a while, to let us both heal further and regain our energy. It's no use attempting to get out of here when we're in this condition." I cup her nose in my hand, getting a nod of agreement. "Hopefully, we won't get another visit from Surt before we can try to escape."

Are you going to give me any hint of what you're planning? One scaly eyebrow rises as interest dances in her eyes.

I shake my head. "Not yet. I'm not proud of what I'm thinking, but I'm out of ideas. Also, I don't want to say it out loud, just in case the lava monster can hear everything I've got planned. I'd hate to give them a warning and possibly ruin our last chance."

I guess I better get healing then.

Even though I'm nearly spent, I pump the last of

my healing energy into her soft nose for an overall heal then curl up against her side, keeping my healing leg stretched forward. Elan's breathing slows to an even rhythm, lulling her into relaxation.

Fixing my gaze on the lava river, I watch the molten lava flow past. Despite our situation, the orange-red glow holds a certain allure, bringing beauty to the dry, desolate realm. Elan lowers her head closer to my body, resting it on her front talons. I drape an arm over her front leg.

"You know, despite lava being scalding hot and dangerous, something is mesmerizing about that river. To some extent, it brightens this place. Perhaps it's the call of death. I don't know."

Elan suddenly straightens and glares at me. *Dragon scales! What are you talking about? It sounds like you're longing for death.*

I nudge her with my shoulder. "That's not what I meant, Elan. You know that."

Chapter Fourteen

B eads of sweat form on my brow and trickle into my eyes, the salty water blurring my vision. I wipe the moisture from my forehead with an arm, cursing this dreadful heat. The realm of Muspelheim lacks the abundance of fresh air, and being trapped in this hot cave with the entrance blocked accelerates my yearning for freshness. Getting back to Midgard, with its large green trees and oxygen-filled air, would bring me great joy. I wipe my brow again, but with the sweat coating my arm, the gesture proves useless.

Elan's gaze bores into me, and I meet her stare.

So are you going to tell me what your next move is? Elan's voice is a welcome distraction, easing the discomfort of the heat.

Bending one knee, I embrace my good leg, leaving the splinted one straight. "To be honest, I can't do anything until your wing heals. No matter what I have planned, I don't think anyone's going to get you very far in your condition... unless a giant rescues us." I chortle softly, my voice remaining in a whisper. "I don't know about you, but I don't know of any giants friendly enough to help us."

Folding my bent leg to the side, I reach forward and jab at my broken leg, testing for any tenderness. Even when I poke my leg roughly where the bone once protruded from my skin, it remains free from pain. After untying the straps securing the sword to my leg, I remove the sheath and tuck it back into its home between my back and the quiver.

Tugging my mended leg close, I rest the bent knee against the other, folding my legs in a zigzag as I lean on my right hip.

Happy that I can bend my leg again, I study Elan. "How's your wing feeling? And don't lie about it. I need to know your proper condition."

She stretches to one side then pushes off the ground to stand. After rising to my feet, I circle her large form to reach the wounded wing.

My fingers trace the bones, feeling for any remaining breaks and studying Elan's face for any sign of pain. I poke a couple of places where I remember bad breaks. "You're looking a lot better. I guess my magic helped because you weren't embedded with whatever magic the first lava monster tainted you with."

Elan unfurled her wings, extending them wide, and flapped them a few times, just enough to test their strength but remaining grounded.

A grin spreads across her face, displaying her nasty-looking teeth. *It feels much better. I'll give it a few more hours before giving them another go with more force. If we decide it's at full strength then, you need to put your plan into place.* A cheeky smirk spreads over her face. *I don't know why you think people can't carry me out of here. I'm only small.*

I quirk an eyebrow, acknowledging her cheekiness. "The only thing you're small against is giants."

She stops flapping and lowers her wings, and I take the opportunity to inject more healing magic into her body and old wounds.

Elan hums with pleasure as I run my hands down the joints and bones. *That feels so good. I think I'll be able to fly again very soon.*

My hands buzz with the release of magic. "That's good. But it would be best if you didn't rush it. I want to make sure you feel capable."

Elan stops flapping, drops to her stomach, and rests her head on her front feet. I circle to her other side and drop to the ground, snuggling in against her again, soaking up her company.

Do you think Thor will come? Elan asks. *I was hoping he would be here by now.*

"I don't think so." I shift my weight to my other side, taking pressure off my healing leg. "I think he's still passed out or Odin's stopping him. Secretly, I hope he would go against Odin, at least to help us out of here, but I can't be sure. I don't think Thor would leave me here if he knew we were in danger, but who knows? He's always shown me more care than Odin ever has."

What about Mistress Sigrun? Her attitude has changed a lot over the last couple of years.

I run my hands down my forearms, wiping off some of the accumulated sweat. "Yes, but she also follows Odin's rules, and he's banished me. So I'm pretty sure she won't help me."

Elan straightens, tension hardening her body. *Even after everything you've done? Not even to get you out of danger?*

Heaviness weighs on my shoulders as I shake my head. "I doubt it."

What about Anita? Would she be able to help? I know she would if she could.

"I don't think she would be able to get away

unnoticed. Her healing talent is in demand. Besides, I'd have to get Ratatoskr back. Something tells me he isn't going to visit anytime soon. Unless, by some chance, someone sends me another message."

A loud squawking pierces the eeriness of the fire realm. Elan turns invisible, and I squat low to the ground, peering out the large opening facing the lava river. Something glides across the entrance, the dark form illuminated by the background of molten stone. The creature has long pointy wings and a thin extended neck finished with a long beak. The shape and size of the creature reminds me of a pterodactyl that existed in prehistoric times on Midgard—one of the many animals I read about in the strange creatures' section of the academy library at the time I was searching for information about the zmey. Shivers run down my spine as I remember the lava dragon we encountered not long before, and I wonder what exotic gifts this creature may have.

The birdlike creature flies in a straight line, only pumping its wings every few yards to break up the smooth glide, enough to keep it at the same level. I press farther into the ground, attempting to flatten myself against the rocks. If this creature is hungry, I don't want to be its next meal. If it's anything like the rest of the animals in this land, it's probably also vicious. We keep our eyes on the creature until it finally disappears in the distance.

Elan turns visible. *That creature looks nasty. I could take it on, but I don't need any more injuries.* The scales along her snout bunch together as she screws up her face. *We need to get out of here.*

Pushing against the ground, I rise to a seating position. "I completely agree."

If we get out of here—she catches my scowl—*or should I say, when, where are you going to go? I could sneak you into the dragon wastelands. It's part of Asgard, but I doubt Odin would come to find you there.*

I groan. "I don't know. I have to find Loki, but he could be on Asgard, hiding in plain sight of the gods. That would make it tricky for me to find him." I lean against Elan's side and straighten my legs, crossing one over the other. "I'll work it out when I get out of here. One step at a time, as they say."

She nudges my legs with her nose. *I know for sure that Mother will protect you. And of course, I will too.*

"Thanks, Elan. Let's see how it goes. Maybe Loki has left Asgard by now."

Her concerned eyes study me. *What do you think his plan is?*

Confused, I frown. "What do you mean?"

In one instance, he's giving you the power of magic, then the next, he's betraying you. On top of that, it's happened again. He seemed to help you by healing me. Then he looks as though he has betrayed you again, like in this case. I'm pretty sure that he had Ratatoskr tell Surt that you have access to Freya, putting you in more trouble. Elan stands, leaving me fighting to regain my balance after pulling my support away. The scales on her brow crumple together in a frown. *He helped you on your trip to Jotunheim, but now he's leaving you to rot in Muspelheim, yet you haven't done anything different to him. It doesn't make sense.* She paces in front of me, her talons clicking on the rocks. *Is he on our side or against us?*

I stand, leaning on my better leg. "I don't know. I want to think he's with us, but his actions often confuse me, just like you say. He did help me a lot when I was fighting to prove that wingless Valkyries were worth more than slaves. Yet at the same time, he went through all that effort to raise the dragon army and used them to rise against us. It is confusing." My boots crunch on the rocks as I join Elan in pacing. "Right now, my focus is to clear my name and recapture him if I can't convince him to do the right thing. Then there's the problem of his children. If he's recaptured, they'll probably act up again." I halt and flail my arms in frustration. "It's like Asgard is in trouble either way. But I can't help Asgard while I'm banished. Not properly, anyway."

A dark strand of hair hangs over my face, and I tuck it behind my ear. "We can deal with the children one by one. I'm also confused about their involvement. We thought Hel was attacking Asgard, but so far, she isn't. She didn't send the lava monster."

Elan stops pacing and plunks to the ground, expelling a groan of frustration. *Nope. It seems like Surt sent the monster to attack us.*

Imitating her actions, I rest against her side. "You know, it's pretty pathetic. How are you supposed to win over a bride-to-be by forcing others to give up her location?" I rest my head against Elan's scales and glare at the lava monster's legs, still dangling over the river entrance of the cave.

We sat in silence. Elan's golden eyes stare longingly out the opening until her eyelids grow heavy and she dozes. The sight of the legs keeps burning anger surging within my stomach, and my mind spins as I consider how I got here and ponder my next move. My eyes constrict with determination. I don't want to put anyone else in danger or get them in trouble with Odin and kicked out of Asgard. I only have one plan of action that I think might work, and no matter how I look at it, that would still bring the person into danger if we're not careful—if my call for help would even work.

I long to grasp the thing that could give me a link

to the outside world. It may not work. I know it's grasping at straws, but I'm desperate. The option is my last and final hope. With only two of us against the lava monster and the other weird creatures of Muspelheim, I can't see us successfully escaping this realm alone.

Eventually, Elan's breathing staggers as she yawns then clicks her tongue against the top of her mouth and extends her front legs in an exaggerated stretch. *What did I miss?*

I chuckle. "Absolutely nothing."

She grins, her eyes still drooping with drowsiness. *Good to know I didn't stay awake for that.* Slowly, she rises to her feet, giving me enough time to move off her. *I think it's time to check my wings. They feel fabulous.*

Rising to my feet, I stand aside and watch her stretch her legs in a doggy pose with her backside up and her front legs extended straight forward. She then kicks her back legs behind herself, one at a time, rolling her back feet in slow stretches. After shaking her body, she extends her wings, furling then unfurling them. *Yup. I feel awesome. Nothing hurts. Let's give it a go.*

She flaps her wings several times, flying within the cave and circling the widest part. My excitement rises, and I want to yell my congratulations. Instead, I wait until she lands to whisper them quietly. I don't want to attract the attention of the lava monster.

Softly, I clap. "That's awesome, Elan."

She leans forward and tilts her head sideways, raising a scaly eyebrow. *Okay. Now I want to see what your trick is. How can we get help?*

Chapter Fifteen

The arrows rattle inside my quiver as I slide it off my back. Holding it in one hand, I stand close to Elan, who lowers her head to press her ear close to my face.

"We have to do this quietly. Don't get your hopes up too much. This may not work, but it's the only thing I can think of, and it may be our last chance of getting help out of here."

She tilts her head to look at me with one of her golden eyes. *At the moment, I'm willing to give anything a try. If it doesn't work, it doesn't work. At least we've given it a go.*

"Okay," I whisper and back away from her slightly to lower my quiver to the ground. The sword attached to it clanks as the hilt hits the stones, synchronizing with the arrows' clatter. I haven't taken it off the whole time we've been in Muspel-heim. Although it's uncomfortable to wear all the time, I never knew what would happen next. Even though my weapons didn't do any good against Surt or the lava monster, they were like a security blanket, and if by some chance we did escape, I didn't want to leave them behind.

"I don't know if you remember, but Freya gave me this." Keeping my voice as low as possible, I squat, clasping the small charm that dangles from the side of my quiver. The charm covers not much more than a fingertip. I hold it between an index finger and thumb, showing off the shiny silver wings with a horn in the center.

Elan peers down at it. *It's pretty. What does it do?*

"At first, I thought it was just a kind gesture by Freya because I didn't have wings, and I badly wanted to prove myself back then. She gave it to me when she had me kidnapped and taken to her camp."

Elan snorts. *Ah. Not exactly the best way to start a friendship.*

I smile. "I know. I guess it wasn't really kidnapping. Let's just say I was roughly escorted to her camp with Mistress Sigrun's approval."

I remember you telling me about it. That was a terrible act by the mistress.

"As it turns out, she had her reasons and gave me this. This little charm has magical powers. It's through this that I called her when we were in the middle of the battle on Asgard."

Elan sniffs the charm. *I don't remember seeing it.*

"You were too busy fighting to know what I did."

How does it work?

Rocks crumble around us, and I check the hole above to make sure the lava monster isn't listening. When I'm confident that it was just shifting to a more comfortable spot, I continue whispering.

"I'm not quite sure. All I do is this." I rub my thumb gently over the charm a couple of times.

Elan tilts her head to one side, her eyes curious. *And then what?*

"And then we wait and see if it still works. I haven't used it since that day and Asgard. There's been no need to."

Nervous, I busy myself with pacing the cave and checking for any fallen arrows I may have missed collecting earlier. The charm remains between my forefinger and thumb as I slump to my backside in the middle of the cave. Elan's eyes barely leave me as she continues circling, her talons tapping on the rocks with each step.

We wait and wait. Nothing happens. I lower myself to my back, the stones poking into my flesh as I gaze up at the covered hole. Worry twists in my stomach, making me sick. The silence eats at me, and

I need all my willpower not to hurl the charm across the cave.

"Maybe it doesn't work anymore."

Sadness fills Elan's eyes. *Maybe it will take a while for her to respond. As you said, you haven't used it for a long time. Perhaps she's forgotten about it, or whatever helps her hear your call is placed aside.* She shrugs, spreading her wings.

"That's not very encouraging," I retort.

She purses her lips. *I'm trying.*

My shoulders cave. "I know." Staring at the little charm, I lightly brush my thumb over it again. "Maybe you're right. Maybe she's lost whatever it is that can tell her I've used it. I don't know for certain, though. I thought the notification happened in her head."

Elan eyes me strangely. *What makes you think that?*

"Because when I accidentally stroked it in front of her, she said it sent a sharp pain through her head from a loud piercing noise." I continue rubbing my thumb softly over the surface, wishing she would hear it. All my hopes collapse with each unanswered stroke. I reach for my quiver bag, ready to put the charm away, when something clicks inside my head, almost like audio has been flicked on. My spine straightens with apprehension.

Kara. You can stop rubbing that thing, please. An

implored urgency underlines the soft, smooth voice inside my head. *I heard you the first time.*

I cringe. "Sorry. I thought you didn't hear me."

I know. My response took so long because I couldn't work out where you were. I need to locate you to talk to you. Where are you, exactly? Murk disturbed the channel, blocking the direct link to wherever you are.

With my head angled toward my lap, I talk to my stomach, trying not to let the lava giant hear or see what I'm doing. "I've been abducted with Elan."

Upon hearing me communicating with someone, Elan stands over me. "Is that—"

I shush her instantly, holding up a palm. "I'm stuck in Muspelheim, the land of the fire giants," I tell Freya.

Her voice is as lovely as I remember it, if not more so. *You're stuck in the land of the fire giants?*

"Yes. We need help to get out of here."

What about Thor? I hear you're serving under him now.

"Thor was rendered unconscious by the lava monster that kidnapped us. He tried to stop it, but it overcame him. He's only one god. I don't know if he's still unconscious or awake. I don't think Ratatoskr has passed on my message."

I haven't had the best communication success with

that little rodent. Her voice fills with distrust. *He delivers what he wants to.*

"I've only known him for a little while, and I'm starting to think that too. Although if what he says is true, Odin has banished me. That means I'm out of luck, trying to get help from Odin."

Why did he banish you? Was it because... Wait. Don't bother. I can ask you later. I'm guessing you have no one else to contact. That's why you've tried me.

"Yes. Are you able to come help us?" I ask, almost pleading.

I'll see what I can do.

The connection wavers, and I fret she's going to break communication before I've finished.

Quickly, I call out, "Wait! Don't you come." I pause, waiting to see if she's gone.

Why? Confusion laces her voice.

I blurt out, "Surt kidnapped me because he wants to find you."

Find me? Her voice is alarmingly seductive and beautiful yet full of surprise.

"Yes. It's something to do with him wanting you to be his wife."

Her chuckle is priceless, filled with a deep sensuality bubbling from the depths of her abdomen. When she finally regains composure, she says, *That's delirious but also not good news. Leave it with me, and I'll see what I can do. I won't come unless I have to.* The bond in my head severs, leaving me feeling empty, with a blank open space.

I gaze at Elan, feeling slightly more relaxed.

What was that? Elan's voice fills the space in my head.

"She contacted me." I refrain from using Freya's name, just in case the lava monster can hear me.

Elan executes a little happy dance with her front talons. *That's great news! So what took so long?*

"She said she had trouble because the connection was all hazy and she had to push through some barrier. Perhaps Muspelheim is out of reach from where she usually communicates."

Is she going to help?

"She's working on it. Hopefully, that means she'll organize someone else to come and get us—more than one person, I hope. I don't know who she knows besides her army of angels of death. I doubt they'll come—they hate Valkyries. I guess we'll just have to wait and see."

- Chapter Sixteen -

The wait for a rescue party drags on. With each passing minute, the creeping tentacles of worry wrap around me, squeezing every particle of optimism from my pores. Maybe the rescue party can't make it. It probably hasn't been as long as I think, but again, telling time in Muspelheim is proving difficult. I miss the sun rising and setting or even the sky changing from darkness to light.

My worry and restlessness make me want to pace, but resisting the urge is essential in case it leads the lava monster to think something is amiss. I don't know who to expect. I hope Freya keeps her promise and doesn't come personally because that would expose her to the danger of being spotted by Surt. Not only do I not want that, but she's also my only hope for us being rescued.

My impatience nibbles at me, calling me to rub my thumb over the charm again. If I do it, finding out what's happening might ease my mind. Still, I resist the urge. Giving in could hinder the whole process and affect the outcome.

Instead, I take deep breaths to calm my nerves and mantra myself into thinking everything will be okay. The positivity is hard to retain as I stare out at the monster's dangling legs, partially blocking the way to the river.

As though picking up on my thoughts and restlessness, Elan angles her face toward me, her outline softened by affection. *Get some sleep, little one.*

I chortle. "What are you, my mother?"

She chuckles, turning her soft eyes on me. *In this instance, I think I should be. You're tired, Kara. You need to get some sleep.*

Worry creases my brow, and I fix my eyes on the glowing lava.

Elan insists, *Go on. Worrying won't help. It'll only make you more exhausted and unable to function properly.* She follows my line of sight then studies me again. *I'll keep an eye out.*

She's right. I couldn't do anything even if something came to attack us. Although I could try to defend us with my magic and my tiny weapons. I curl into a fetal position between Elan's front legs. I doubt anything I could do would help, and I am exhausted to the bone from having healed myself and Elan.

She nudges me softly with her nose. *That's it. I'll wake you if anything happens.*

Just knowing Elan is beside me and keeping an eye on things brings me some peace. Uncurling slightly, I lay my head on her front leg then cup my hands, resting my face on them and wriggling slightly to get comfortable. "Okay. But wake me at the first sign of danger. Or if anything happens."

I will. She brushes her lips against my face, which feels like the comforting kiss of a mother. *Relax. Get some rest. If someone does come, you're going to need your energy.*

In a matter of seconds, my eyes close, and I pull my knees closer to my chest, allowing my breath to slow. The needed sleep is overcome by strange dreams and haunted by an enormous lava monster and fire giant. Strong smells of sulfur are eventually overcome by the smell of rotting flesh, pushing my thoughts back to the times on Midgard when we were fighting the angels of death. Even in my dreams, I realize that hoping the angels of death would come is wishful thinking. More likely is the possibility that I've been dragged into the depths of Helheim. I imagine it's filled with the smell of rotting corpses even though I haven't been there. After all, that's where the dead without an honorable death go. Then again, maybe just the souls occupy it, not the bodies.

The smell grows stronger, overwhelming my senses until I can no longer smell anything else. A warm breeze brushes over my face, chilling the accumulated sweat. The coolness lures me from my light sleep, and I crack my eyelids. Wing shapes framed against the lava river background flutter before me, and I blink, attempting to clear my vision. The shapes remain, and I pry my eyes open farther.

Between the wings hang human male forms. After prying a hand from under my face, I rub my eyes to remove my hallucination. When it doesn't budge, I push myself upright and stare.

At first, fear rises within me. Every muscle tenses as I brace myself, ready to defend us with Elan's help. Then I realize it's a swarming flock of angels of death. Two of them fly in together. Between them hangs a strong male form with bulging muscles and no wings. The two angels of death sway as though unbalanced by his bulk.

Something is familiar about this man, and I watch their descent until they land with an ungraceful thud.

Excitement overcomes me as I rise to my feet. This must be Freya's rescue party. She must've sent them. Even though I know she instructs the dark warrior angels, I'm surprised they've come. They're the Valkyries' long-time enemies.

The human that had hung between them charges toward me.

Conscious that the lava monster is still above us, I say in a voice not much louder than a whisper, "Beowulf?"

He stands straight, crosses his forearms, and thumps his fists twice on his chest. "In the flesh."

I cringe at the level of his voice but smirk. This was how he greeted my friends and me when we first encountered him, and it made us laugh. We thought he was rather weird. However, he also saw us as the enemy then because we were riding our monstrous beasts, the dragons.

More angels of death fly into the cave, their faces serene and their landings soft.

Gazing upward, I watch to see if the monster shows any signs of knowing they're here. When his backside doesn't move, I return my attention to Beowulf and whisper, "What are you doing here? How did you know about this rescue party?"

"I'm Beowulf. Slayer of all monst—" His voice is still too loud, and instantly, the two angels of death that escorted him each slap a hand over his mouth, stopping his words while shushing him.

A frustrated expression crosses Beowulf's face

before it flattens in resignation. When they pull their hands away from his mouth, this time, he keeps his voice in a whisper. "I'm here to guide them in slaying the monsters. It's not their usual job. Because of this, and seeing they don't have magic, Freya asked me to come along." His eyes turn dreamy. "I would do anything for that goddess."

I roll my eyes and slap him on the back. "Thanks for coming, Beowulf. And thank you all for coming." I turn to the rest of the angels of death, their number close to thirty. "I didn't think that you would come. I'm very grateful."

One of the black-clothed angels moves to the middle of the group, his shoulders slightly broader than the rest. He seems to be the leader. "We understand that you've been taken hostage because of your connections with Freya." When I incline my head, he continues, "For this reason, we will come even though Valkyries are normally enemies."

My voice is husky when I answer, "Thank you."

Freya has risked a lot more of her soul reapers than I expected. I've seen how she mourns over them if they're lost.

I ask, "How did you know where to find me?"

An amused expression crosses the face of the leader. He spreads his legs, dressed in long black pants, and crosses his arms over his black top.

"Freya can track you by that charm she gave you. Did you think it was only so you could call her?"

I drop my gaze to the ground, feeling slightly stupid. "That would make sense, that she could track it as well as hear me. She's probably been keeping an eye on me these last couple of years."

My hinting is ignored with a one-sided smirk. "The goddess says if she taps into it properly, she can not only hear the charm, she can also find out where you are. It helps more when she knows what realm you're in."

Gazing at my quiver, I examine the charm. It looks innocent and inconspicuous, yet it can do so much. I'm tempted to rub the wings as I marvel at the brilliance, but I resist. "That's a lot of things this pretty little charm can achieve. How does that work?"

He shrugs. "I have no idea. But she's a goddess after all, and her magic abounds."

Pulling my attention away from the charm, I search their faces. Sadness crashes in my stomach at the memory of their past leader, Cael. I finally managed to win him over slightly, only to have him ripped away as he defended us in a battle against the dark elves. Also, Loki used the guise of an angel of death to befriend me. That was one of many times I trusted someone who turned out to be Loki in another form.

Quickly, I push these thoughts aside. From my trip to Freya's camp, I recognize some familiar faces in this small group, who fought by our side to protect Asgard. As I study their faces, I notice they all, including Beowulf, have large spears strapped to their backs and swords hanging at their sides. I don't know how well these weapons will work at getting us out of here, but I can only hope it will be enough with this many.

"Thank you again for coming..." I give the leader a questioning look.

He straightens his shoulders. "Ander. My name is Ander."

I smile at the start of this relationship. "What's the plan?" I ask, keeping my voice extra low.

His black eyes study Elan. "Can your dragon carry two riders?"

"Yes."

Ander narrows his eyes. "I've heard that she can also turn invisible. Is this correct?"

"Yes. But I don't have my cloak that can turn me invisible." I expel a disappointed sigh. "The monster is probably keeping an extra-diligent eye out for me trying to get out, more than anything else."

Rocks clatter around us, and I freeze, urgently whispering, "Take cover!"

Suddenly, all the angels of death squat and spread their black wings over their bodies. The two closest to Beowulf slam him to the ground and cover him and themselves with their black wings.

As the rocks continue to fall, I place a magical barrier above the strange-smelling angels to protect them from the tumbling stones. The legs at the river opening move away as the hole above opens and more rocks clatter around us.

Glaring at the hole above, I make sure Elan and I remain within view as a burning ember eye stares down at us.

My breath hitches in my throat, and Elan's does the same as we wait to see what the lava monster does. It continues to peer down as though it heard something. I don't know if the beast did hear something or if it's just conducting a checkup, but the pupil-less eye seems too curious for comfort.

With careful concentration, I maintain a blank expression so that the monster can't read my emotions. I'm still not sure just how smart these things are.

The cave around me lies motionless except for the disgruntled snorting of Elan. The efforts of the angels of death are laudable. Their ability to lie entirely still for so long while keeping the robust Beowulf stationary, protected, and quiet is a feat. The brazen Beowulf seems to have a short attention span, and he'll be itching to attack this monster. He doesn't seem deterred that it's much larger than a dragon.

Although the black-clothed angels are deathly still, I can't abolish that stench of rotting corpses, and I hope the sulfur masks it from the monster's sense of smell. Perhaps the molten material inside the beast destroys all scent. That would make sense.

The lava monster keeps peering down at us, and I make a show of sitting by Elan's side and resting my head against her. My tension rises as time ticks by slowly, seconds seeming like hours as I return the gaze of the fiery monster. I hope the angels of death can keep still for a while longer. Stretching my legs out, I cross them at the ankles, hooking one boot over the other as I feign casual boredom.

The beast's attention lingers too long, and I fear that the monster has heard my visitors. Beowulf wasn't exactly quiet a couple of times.

Picking up a rock from beside my leg, I throw it across the cave, allowing a deep grunt to escape with the effort. I do this a few times under the monster's curious glare, making sure my grunts are deep enough to be a man's.

Still sensing the glowing eyes on me, I stare into those pits and call out, "Did I disturb you?" I shrug and huff a laugh. "Sorry. I'm still here, and so's my dragon." I toss a few more stones, repeating the deep grunts.

Eventually, the lava monster pulls back, and the whole body shifts, causing rocks to fall on us as it covers the top hole and hangs its legs over the side entrance. Again, I block the stones from falling on the dark angels, who remain as still as death on the ground, and send the fallen rocks back to their original places, just as Gilroma taught me a couple of years ago.

When I'm sure we're no longer being watched, I whisper to the nearest angel, "I think it's all good now."

His handsome face, framed with long black hair, gazes up at me with uncertainty in his eyes.

"You can move," I whisper.

Slowly, the angels of death stand, their black eyes assessing the visible parts of the lava monster, ready to react again if need be.

Released from the embrace of the angels, Beowulf climbs to his feet. "These beasts are hideous." A mischievous smirk fills his face, but he's finally keeping his voice soft. "Now, there's a challenge to defeat, even a little scary, but I'm willing."

Shaking my head, I touch Beowulf on the back. "Let's hope it doesn't come to that. I'd rather sneak out than take on a monster from this realm."

Ander approaches with the bearing of a leader. "As you can see, when we cover ourselves with our black wings, that hides us in this dark realm. It will be best if you and Beowulf ride your dragon in her invisible form. Many of us will hover around you both, with our wings spread. Hopefully, this will block the view of you sitting on your dragon."

I raise my eyebrows. "Sounds risky."

One half of Ander's mouth lifts into a wry smile. "And staying here is not?"

Thinking that I've accidentally insulted my rescuers, I quickly say, "Oh no, I didn't mean anything by it." I rub an upper arm, pushing my eyebrows together. "Yes, you're right. Everything sounds risky." My words come out in a rush.

There's something about these angels of death with their high, smooth cheeks, firm jaws, and tanned skin that makes me nervous when talking to them. Although they are the Valkyries' enemies, they are somewhat handsome, almost like each is the other half of a Valkyrie, her matching male rival. All the Valkyries are females, while the angels of death are all males. It's a shame the smell of corpses shrouds them.

Attempting to change my line of thought before I embarrass myself, I turn to Beowulf. "Are you ready?"

He smirks. "I was born ready."

Pulling on Elan's scales, I slowly climb onto her back. At times like this, I miss the saddle I made for her. I have ridden her bareback, but I wonder how Beowulf will do. Once I'm up, I reach over the side and assist Beowulf, yanking him up by the collar of his tunic. He slips and slides while attempting to grab Elan's scales, which brings a smile to my face.

After a final pull, he manages to hook one leg over her back and lever himself up into a sitting position, then he shimmies forward to wrap his arms around my waist.

Several angels of death surround us. I'm not sure how they will pull this plan off, but we don't have any other choice, as Ander said. Their faces are focused, their expressions set in determination as though ready to tackle their next mission.

When my eyes connect with the leader's, Ander whispers, "Are you ready?"

Keeping my mouth shut, I nod.

He moves closer to make sure I can hear him. "Get your dragon to fly out in her invisible form, and a couple of us will hover over you. Hopefully, this will block the lava monster from seeing you and Beowulf."

"Let's do this," I say.

Changing into her invisible form, Elan pushes

into the air and slowly flies toward the river entrance. Her pace is slow enough to give the angels time to keep up and hover above us with their black wings, which I can't help but be mesmerized by. From birth, I've always had a fascination with wings. They're so beautiful, and I feel a slight pang of jealousy churn within me—just like when I watch the winged Valkyries. The black wings of these angels of death are as beautiful as the Valkyries' white ones. Even though I now have Elan, who acts as my wings, my life would have been much easier if I was born with my own.

We exit the cave under the cover of the angels' wings and quickly cross the river, away from the glowing red lava. The dark wings wouldn't be incognito with a glowing background. We're better off flying over the dark land, where their wings have a better chance of blending in.

After reaching the far side, we follow the edges of the river. Many more angels of death surround us, their wings beating in an alternating synchronization, providing us with more shelter. I manage to catch a small glimpse of the cave, and the tension in my shoulders releases slightly when I see the monster still sitting on top, seemingly oblivious to our escape. Full of gratitude, I gaze at my rescuers' faces and long, flowing black hair. Viewing them as my rescuers doesn't detract from how handsome each one is, dressed in all black, with powerful black wings.

I marvel at our escape, realizing that Freya was quite smart to send these dark heroes to come and get us. I hadn't realized how their black wings and uniforms and hair would benefit us in this land. Freya must've known of the nature of this place. I hope to the gods that she hasn't been here or let her knowledge of the realm become known to Surt. That would just encourage him.

Under the dark warriors' protection, we manage to travel quite a distance in a short period. I don't know where we're going, but I assume they do. They only recently arrived and weren't blindfolded or kidnapped when they did.

The angels seem to be heading in a specific direc-tion, with Ander leading the way. We accelerate to a speed that indicates they must know where they are going. They seem to have a homing mechanism leading them back to the entrance. I gaze over my shoulder and catch another glimpse of the cave in the distance. We have traveled quite far, and the monster hasn't pursued us. With each beat of Elan's wings, my hope rises. Perhaps we will get out of here without being missed.

The lava river swerves to the right, and we dive

toward the ground as Elan follows Ander and a few other angels of death. As we maintain a height several feet from the ground, I wonder why, for we don't seem to have a reason for the descent. I'm about to ask, thinking of a diplomatic way to question the leader, when Elan swerves to the right and lowers farther. Suddenly, a loud spine-tingling roar reverberates across the desolate and burning blackstone countryside.

- Chapter Eighteen -

A chill settles into my bones. The sensation is strange as my skin is slick with sweat from the heat of the fire realm. That roar sounds familiar. The cover from the angels of death parts slightly as each one twists to find the source of the cry.

At first, the blackened fields behind us seem vacant—not a pair of lava-filled eyes to be seen anywhere. But suddenly, about ten feet behind us, the river springs to life and sucks the lava from the riverbed as a sizeable gaping jaw rises from it.

Dragon scales! Elan pulls up, bringing us out of the protective barrier of the angels of death, who remain behind, too stunned by the sight of the creature forming before them to move quickly. *It's the lava dragon.*

Beowulf's voice croaks behind me. "It's the what?"

Peering over my shoulder, I meet his wide eyes.

Even the slayer of monsters is stunned by this creature. "It's a dragon that forms out of the lava river. We encountered it when we tried to escape." I gaze back at the angels, who still haven't moved yet. "Go! Fly!" I scream.

My demand seems to knock away their shock, and they jolt into action, flapping their wings and darting upward, away from the creature-forming river.

We're too late. The dragon forms quickly, its figure shooting toward them with its mouth open wide. It devours one of the angels of death, snapping its jaws shut.

"Mother of Midgard!" Beowulf curses behind me.

I'm jerked from behind as my Valkyrie fighting leathers are grasped at the back of my neck.

Turning, I see Beowulf has risen to his feet, his spear set ready in his spare hand. He hurls it at the dragon, the action yanking at my uniform. Thankfully, the front of my uniform doesn't rise to my neck, or it would have choked me.

The maneuver causes him to slide.

I slip on Elan's back and clench my legs harder around her neck as I grasp her scales, feeling their sharp edges bite into my flesh. "Beowulf. Sit down!"

The spear aims straight for the dragon's enormous chest, disappearing into the crawling molten skin with a slight burst of flame as the wooden shaft catches aflame.

"Argh!" Beowulf's disappointed grunt attracts the attention of the lava dragon.

Beowulf, sit! Elan commands.

With a huff, Beowulf does as he's told just before Elan rapidly changes direction, aiming higher, away from the gaping maw of the enormous dragon.

Looking over my shoulder, I watch as the angels of death throw their spears at the dragon's heart, or where the heart should be, as though following Beowulf's guidance. Each one of the spears combusts into flames.

The dragon rises up and up, the dark pits of its eyes following our progress. Suddenly, Beowulf yanks my sword from its sheath on my back and throws it at the dragon. I use my magic to aim it at the beast's temple, hoping that the metal doesn't disintegrate as his spear did. I've grown rather attached to my flying sword.

For a human, Beowulf's throw is strong, and my sword shoots straight through the lava dragon's head and exits the other side. The dragon roars in frustration as the strike aggravates the dragon rather than killing it.

"Can this thing die?" Bewilderment laces Beowulf's voice.

Shaking my head, I hold out my hand, calling to my sword and happy that it hasn't melted. "I don't know. Why did we fly so low in the first place?"

Beowulf points at a location on the ground. "Because this is where we entered Muspelheim."

Following his finger, I spot Ander disappearing into a hole below, followed by a few angels of death.

"Then we need to follow if we can avoid the dragon." Worried that my sword is still hot, I magically instruct it to follow, and its tiny wings flap, hovering nearby. "Do you think we can make it through that hole, Elan, before the dragon blocks our way?"

I shall try.

Several more angels of death give us one final glance before disappearing into the hole. Their eyes are wide, and they look ready to leave this horrid realm as soon as possible. They cast a last glimpse into the realm, seemingly to make sure I've seen where they're disappearing. A few dark warriors remain floating around the lava dragon, trying to keep the dragon occupied for a little longer.

Another roar sounds in the distance, and I pull my attention away from the lava dragon. Over the mountains with cascading lava waterfalls, Surt stomps toward us. His massive lava-filled mouth opens as he roars again. Even in the distance, the large horns circling out of his head are intimidating, framed by smaller circular horns. His burning red eyes glare in our direction as he realizes his pawn to lure Freya here is escaping. I'm amazed that those eyes without pupils can see so far.

My attention falls toward the hole, growing smaller beneath us as Elan rises to avoid another attack from the lava dragon. "We need to get out of here, Elan. As soon as you get a chance, dash for the hole even if it makes our ride difficult. We'll just have to hang on."

Without needing instruction, Beowulf wraps his hands tightly around my waist, and I feel his legs tighten around Elan's frame. My knuckles are already white from hanging onto her scales, but I tighten my grasp anyway.

Elan's speed increases, and I feel a rush of hot air as the dragon's jaws clamp shut, narrowly missing us. Suddenly, Elan flips to the side and dives. The lava dragon is too slow to catch us in its mouth. Hot air blows over my face, and my cheeks push back from the pressure as she flips, plummeting toward the hole as another angel disappears into it. Taking in the size of the hole, I grow concerned. It's not very big.

"Are you going to fit, Elan?"

Not sure. I'll have to make it work.

The rumbling of giant footsteps grows louder.

Surt is progressing rapidly, his glowing eyes remaining fixed on us. We dodge the swipes of the lava dragon, now twisting to pursue us again.

"Hurry!" I yell. My heart is thumping profusely in my chest, desperate to break free before he closes the gap between us. "Hurry!" I repeat.

Elan flips a couple more times then lands when we reach the hole.

Surt moves closer, his large frame swerving between the last two mountains.

Elan pauses before the hole.

"Go! Go! Go! Go! Go!" I yell in frustration at Elan's immobility.

Surt's footsteps pound the ground harder, the vibrations traveling through my spine as he is nearly upon us. My heart stops beating, and my breath catches in my throat. This must be the end. If we don't leave now, we're done. I wish again that I had wings so I could be the one responsible for my own flight.

The large fire giant stoops from the waist, sweeping his large hand in our direction. My face turns clammy.

When the hand is only a few feet away, Elan cries, *Duck!*

Both Beowulf and I lower toward her back, and she squeezes through the hole, barely making it with us on her back. The space inside is dark, dimly lit by the lava light from Muspelheim. Fortunately, the hole widens inside, allowing Elan to fly through the strange tunnel. It reminds me of the tunnel through Yggdrasil's trunk to Jotunheim.

As Elan steers upward, I suck in an overdue breath as Surt's figure disappears. All my joy at making it through the hole is squashed as the entrance is blocked by a large hand charging through the opening, shaped like a claw and swerving upward.

I yelp then scream, "Go! Go! Go!"

I'm giving it my best, Elan snaps.

I clamp my mouth shut and look ahead to see several sets of black wings blocking out any light shining from a potential escape hole ahead.

"Mother of Midgard!" Beowulf curses, grabbing my attention. He gazes over his shoulder.

A strong breeze blows over my face as the hand swipes, trying to reach farther inside the hole. It jerks to a halt as the length of the arm has reached its limit.

My heart cheers, and facing forward, I concentrate on where we're going. The angels of death pass a portal filled with light. Elan flies past so quickly that I can't get a good look to see what realm the hole may lead to. Eventually, the inside of the tunnel resembles the inside of a trunk of a tree, the walls more wooden rather than stony in appearance, making Muspelheim's part of the Yggdrasil appear burnt out and dead. The beautiful trunk turns into petrified wood.

With each flap of Elan's wings, the heat abates. The pressure slowly seeps away from the back of my shoulders. The headache that had been growing in my temples eases as my stress melts away. I gaze over my shoulder to take in the difference in the World Tree's insides, barely able to make out the stony edges of the hole deep below, where we entered.

Suddenly, we burst through a new hole into a land lush and green, with long flowing rivers full of actual water and sky a color slightly lighter than Naga.

I throw my arms around Elan's neck, hugging her with joy. "This has to be Midgard." I look over my shoulder at Beowulf.

His rugged face is beaming with a smile. "Yes. This is Midgard. I would recognize it anywhere. There's nothing like it."

We rise higher, giving me a perfect view of the sun, which is lowering over the horizon, displaying an impressive array of yellow, orange, red, and blue as the east darkens. The day must be almost over for Midgard, causing me to wonder just how long I was in Muspelheim. As we continue to follow the angels of death, I take in a deep breath, filling my lungs with fresh air, thankful that our flying distance eliminates the angels' odor. The songs of different birds surround us as they settle in for the night. I never grow tired of their beautiful sounds, each bird having an individual tone and song to sing.

Midgard is so beautiful that I could almost live here. Although that's a pleasant thought, it brings me sadness. I must rectify my banishment. Asgard is my home. All my friends are in Asgard, and something tells me I wouldn't fit into Midgard for the rest of my life.

Eventually, we land on soft grass near a large lake. Elan lowers herself, and we climb off. I charge straight for the lake to lap water from my hand like a thirsty animal. I missed food and water in Muspelheim.

When I stand and approach Ander, his face is twisted with grief.

"How many did you lose?" I ask.

The pain in his eyes deepens. "Five."

Sadness rocks my soul. "I'm so sorry." I mutter the useless apology, not knowing what else to say. My gratitude seems dismal in comparison. "Thank you. Thanks so much for saving us. I couldn't have done it without you."

He inclines his head, his face unreadable. His expression is a mask to hide either the pain of loss or his hate of Valkyries. I'm not sure which.

Hoping to get the message through, I reinforce my sympathy. "For what it is worth, I'm so sorry for your loss. I know Freya will be devastated."

His face sharpens.

"I can tell you don't like my kind much. Please know that I and my few wingless friends are not like the other Valkyries. We don't have much to do with the reaping of souls. Although we have taken part in it at times."

His expression stays the same.

"I believe the reaping of souls could be done less aggressively and more fairly. I hope we can be friends to a point. I have much respect for Freya and all the angels of death."

"Noted." The word lacks empathy, a silent reminder that he isn't going to be my friend. He has done his duty, and that is as far as he is going.

My shoulders arch slightly as I release a sigh of defeat. "So what next? Are you taking me to see Freya?"

He shakes his head. "When she's ready, Freya is coming here."

"Oh? Why? Wouldn't it be best if you take me to

her?" I try to sound like I'm not being bossy. "I know she's busy."

"It's easy to blindfold you and Beowulf but not so easy to blindfold your dragon. I know she's an intelligent creature. On top of that, we can't carry her. She's massive. So Freya will be coming here." He nods, clicks his heels, and marches off, leaving me staring at his back.

Hearing the birds chirping in the trees of Midgard shrouds my soul in peace. The sound is comforting and refreshing after having been kidnapped and taken to a place filled with arid ground and lava with a sulfur stench. Muspelheim is a place where everything seems to be burned and dead. Even the fire giants and their creatures are either filled with lava or made from lava.

Heading down to the water's edge again, I splash some water over my face, washing off the grime and sweat I've accumulated during my time in the hot realm. Splashing sounds beside me, and I turn to find Beowulf squatting by my side, washing his arms.

Giving my face one final wipe, I sit down. "Thank you for your help, Beowulf. I'll make sure to tell Thor that you aided me, along with the angels of death."

Beowulf smirks, his eyes turning soft. "I would

do anything for the goddess Freya. Her beauty is something to behold."

I look to the sky, silently pleading for help.

"Don't you roll your eyes at me, young Kara. It is true. It's the first time I've laid my eyes on such beauty." He twists his mouth to one side. "Although I would also rescue you if Thor asked me."

I chortle. "So you wouldn't do it just for me?"

He raises a bushy eyebrow. "Your last visit to Midgard was interesting, to say the least. You and your young Valkyrie friends are good warriors that I would gladly fight beside. It was especially educational for me when you brought your beasts." He glances over his shoulder and nods at Elan. "I've never been so close to a dragon that I wasn't fighting."

Elan's eyes narrow.

Beowulf grins at the golden dragon. "Don't be alarmed. You're my friend. We won't be enemies." He rises to his feet and approaches her. "You're the first creature that I've said that to."

A fire burns in Elan's golden eyes, and she lifts her head and snorts. *You're somewhat self-confident, aren't you, Beowulf? As if you'd have a chance against me as a dragon. I'm appalled that you have attacked any dragon without getting to know them first.*

Beowulf chuckles and elbows me. "She's a feisty one, that one. I think I'm going to like her more than I expected."

Judging by the look in Elan's eye, I have to admire his courage—or perhaps stupidity—when he moves closer to her.

"Don't worry your strange scaly head. After meeting you and your friends, I'll make sure I give dragons the benefit of the doubt before I attack." He leans against her side and crosses his legs. "Although if they attack me first, they're fair game."

Something trickles in the water, and I spring to my feet, backing away from its edge. A scaly brown shape slithers not far from the border of the river.

Beowulf catches sight of the monster and yanks me farther away from the water while backing away. "The Midgard Serpent. He's still restless."

I frown. "I thought Loki's children weren't supposed to be restless anymore."

Beowulf's grip tightens around my upper arm. "Never underestimate Jormungandr," he says. "He's never happy with being peaceful. For as long as I've known, he has always had an evil gleam in his eyes."

The water stirs more, and I'm again surprised at the scaly creature's width when it shows some skin above the surface. The water ripples and swirls with each slithering movement. A chill runs down my spine as it glides past, and I back farther away. We have no guarantee that it won't leave the water and come after us.

"Isn't this a freshwater river?" I ask.

"The ocean must be fairly close to here. It's quite normal for the Serpent to visit some of the rivers that join the ocean," Beowulf says.

A low rumble sounds in Elan's throat as the scales slither closer. Still, the Serpent doesn't move away, unthreatened by a dragon only a fraction of its size. Elan growls again.

With an unexpected flick, the serpent's body kinks, twisting and turning, until beady black eyes rise above the water, followed by the Serpent's nose. The beady eyes move closer, staring us down.

Slowly, as though not to startle the monster, Beowulf moves farther away from the water's edge, pulling me along with him. Jormungandr watches as we make our retreat. The serpent slowly opens its mouth, larger than Elan's body, exposing its long fangs. Black venom drips from the points into the water, and few small fish nearby float to the surface, belly up.

Elan roars, and the beady eyes turn toward her. I want to stand in front of her to protect her, but I know that would do nothing. The distraction gives Beowulf time to dash backward and grab a spear, which he throws at the serpent after a few running steps.

The serpent spots it coming and swirls slightly, and the spear plummets deep into the water as the serpent heads closer to the shore of the river and rises onto the bank. Water drips away from the scales as it slithers farther onto dry land.

We back away while I glance over my shoulder, looking for the angels of death, making sure they're a safe distance away and the path is clear for us to escape. The angels are nowhere to be found.

Sensing Elan edging closer to me, I do the same. Catching Beowulf's attention, I discreetly indicate Elan with my head. He nods once and moves closer, ready to jump onto her back and take flight.

The Serpent continues to edge its way onto the shore, closing on us more quickly than we can move toward each other. I'm bracing myself, ready to run, when a bolt of lightning rises to the sky, forks, and is followed by a loud clap of thunder.

I huff in fascination. Not a single storm cloud was above us earlier. Now in the darkening sky, a large black cloud hovers directly overhead. I jump as another clap of thunder seems to shake the sky, and lightning pierces the ground just in front of the Midgard Serpent's nose.

The Serpent halts, retreats, and flicks itself back into the water in a few seconds. Joy surges within me as those murky brown scales disappear underneath the water.

More forks of lightning hit the ground just behind the Serpent in an additional threat. Judging by how the lightning hit the ground, only one explanation makes sense.

I scan the area and the darkening horizon until I see a figure on top of the mountain. Standing on the pinnacle, Thor clasps Mjolnir and holds it high. Lightning shoots from the hammer into the sky and bounces back to the ground. Another set of lightning forks across the sky in a magnificent display.

My breath catches as relief floods every pore in my body. Thor looks well. Not only that, he has arrived just in time to protect us from the Midgard Serpent.

I call, "Come, Beowulf. Thor's on the mountain. Let's go see him."

We climb onto Elan's back, and she leaps into the sky. She circles the pinnacle, and I spot Thor's two goats and his carriage, parked a small drop from the top. A fresh breeze blows against my face, a welcome change from Muspelheim, and the air grows colder as we climb. Elan lands on the mountainside, not far from Thor, her talons clacking on the rocks.

I jump from her back, Beowulf's thud sounds right behind me, and I scurry to Thor's side.

Chapter Twenty

With excitement coursing through me, I race toward Thor, my spirits rising. Seeing him back to his normal self is fantastic.

I'm baffled to see a vast smirk plastered over his face. My excited footsteps falter, and Thor closes the gap, his grin growing wider. He slaps me on an arm, lurching my thin frame sideways for a couple of steps and ramming me into Beowulf.

"Ha. Ha. Battle maiden. I knew you'd be an interesting companion when I asked for you to be by my side. Especially when things didn't go the way you wanted them to." Still smirking, he places his hands on his hips. "But I didn't think it'd be this entertaining. You've gotten yourself into so much trouble in the last few days. It's quite hilarious."

Regaining my balance, I cross my arms and narrow my eyes. "I'm glad I could entertain you," I say curtly, wobbling my head from side to side. "Nice to see you too."

His smile grows broader as he reads my expression. "There, there." He lightly taps me twice with an open hand on my cheek. "Don't get so upset. You know I love having you around." Then he nudges me with an elbow, and I topple off balance slightly.

I reset my legs in a firmer stance and form my mouth into a thin line.

With amusement twinkling in his eyes, he continues, "It's amazing how much you've been through lately." He feigns thoughtfulness. "Recently, you freed Loki, and then you traveled to Jotunheim to meet Angrboda on Loki's back. You've been kidnapped by a lava monster and taken to Muspelheim then almost eaten by the Midgard Serpent. Have I left anything out?"

"Yeah. Like you failed to save me."

"I saved you this time." His shoulders shake as he chuckles, then he rubs the top of my head as if I were a child.

Shoving his hands away, I move back and scrutinize him. "Yes. At least this time, you succeeded, but last time, you decided to take a little nap instead of rescuing me from the lava monster." Then I smile and fill my voice with warmth. "I'm glad to see you're all better. You had me concerned."

Thor scratches his auburn hair near his temples and looks sheepish. "Hey, I was just unconscious. You were the one kidnapped. Who had who concerned?"

I tilt my head. "Yeah, you were unconscious. Seeing you're the only person who knew I was missing, of course I was concerned."

"Ha. I know you miss me." He peers over my shoulder. "Beowulf. It's nice to see you, my Midgardian brother."

Thor thrusts his hands forward, and the Midgardian follows suit as they clasp each other's forearms and give them a shake.

Thor inclines his head toward me. "Can you see why I keep her around? With all the trouble she gets into, she's extremely entertaining."

Beowulf nods and grins. "Yes, I'm starting to realize. Maybe the Midgard Serpent is attracted to her, and that's the reason it attacked us on the shore before."

A hearty laugh bursts out of Thor, and he throws his head back. "Perhaps you are right. She is an attraction for danger and mischief. Or else I wouldn't have shown such interest in her."

I scowl. "Gee. Thanks a lot." Crossing my arms, I lean on one leg. "Thanks for *trying* to protect Elan and me from the lava monster that kidnapped us. If

I'm only interesting because I attract danger, why were you there in the first place?"

Thor lowers his eyes, a severe expression crossing his face as he adjusts his tunic and shifts his belt around his waist. "I was coming to tell you that my father knew that you let Loki out and that you traveled to Jotunheim with him."

My arms drop to my side. "Oh. Ratatoskr said I was banished. Is this correct?"

Thor's face remains somber as he nods, his blue eyes connecting with mine. "You know Father." He shrugs. "He is very unforgiving if he feels he's been betrayed."

"But I didn't betray him." I wipe my brow on my arm. "I let Loki out, only intending it to be for a few minutes. He was meant to heal Elan and then return. Once again, he backstabbed me."

Thor places a hand on my shoulder. "You know Father isn't going to forgive that."

"Even after everything I've done for Asgard?"

The god of thunder nods. "That seems to be the way it is. We'll have to rectify that somehow."

"How?" I groan. "I can't go into Asgard, and I've no idea where Loki is and what form he's taken. I don't even know it's him if I'm riding him. He can change into too many shapes."

Thor surveys the darkened valleys and the

minimal light remaining over Midgard. The creases on his forehead form dark lines in the dusk. "I will keep an eye on Asgard. But for now, you need protection, and you also need more training with your magic. I've given you much practical training on top of what you've already learned with the Valkyries. Loki has given you a gift, for whatever reason, and you haven't been able to practice or enhance that gift since he's been locked up… except for maybe a few things Anita has taught you about healing."

His eyes look almost sad as they scan the darkening land. "You need to be taught more and have time to practice it."

"And how am I supposed to do that? Where am I supposed to learn more about my magic ability?" I swing my hands out to the sides in exasperation.

His gaze eventually lands on me, his ally even though he's going against his father's approval. "There's a race that deals with magic all the time."

"A race?" I ask. "What do you mean?"

"The whole realm consists of light elves. You should know of it. It's Alfheim."

Annoyance fills me, and I frown. "Yes, of course I know of the realm. But I don't know anyone there who is going to teach me magic."

A soft smile spreads over his face. "You don't

have to find anyone. I have someone that will take you there and will lead you to the right company, someone who can take care of you and nurture you in your time in that realm."

"So I'm going all by myself to a strange realm to learn magic?" I look at him in disbelief. "Somewhere where I know no one, and I'm going with a total stranger."

He slaps a hand onto my shoulder, refraining from his usual force this time. "Oh, Kara. When you say it like that, it sounds dreadful. You won't be alone. You'll be under the good guidance of—"

Beowulf's awestruck voice interrupts us. "Ooh. There she is."

I'd forgotten Beowulf was with us. He gazes dreamily toward the valley, where the angels of death are hovering around a fire.

Chapter Twenty-One

"There who is?" I follow Beowulf's line of sight down to the fire surrounded by angels of death.

Before I can focus, his irritated voice interrupts my thoughts, calling my attention back to him momentarily. His face is barely visible in the twilight. "And who's that male with her?" Beowulf's eyes, filled with admiration only moments before, constrict with annoyance.

My eyes meet Thor's, and amusement dances over his face before he focuses on Beowulf. "My friend, relax. That's Freya's brother, Freyr, not a lover." His smirk grows as he lifts an eyebrow, fixing his blue eyes on Beowulf. "Although I don't think you'll have a chance with Freya."

Beowulf huffs in disgust. "What makes you say that? I'm quite a catch."

Thor arches a bushy auburn eyebrow.

The beast warrior's chin rises, and he puffs out his chest and straightens his back. "I'm quite a catch for a Midgardian. I have big, strong muscles." He flexes, showing off his bulging biceps.

I shake my head. As much as Beowulf has grown on me, he can be a preposterous brute at times.

Thor chuckles and slaps Beowulf on the back. "Yes, my friend, and I do too. But she has her preferences, and it's not you or me."

Trying to distract the drooling males, I attempt a change in conversation. "Why is her brother here?"

Like his sister, Freyr has light blond hair that falls to his shoulders in soft waves.

Thor levels his gaze at me. "He's the friend I was talking about. He's the one that will accompany you to Alfheim and assist you in finding the right trainer for your magic."

"Him?" I squint down at the tall blond male and his white tunic, open at the front and exposing his chest.

He lurks close to Freya, his movements fluid yet bold and confident, oozing a smooth sexuality.

I swallow. "Why him?"

Thor shrugs as though it should be obvious. "He's a friend of mine. On top of that, he's a peaceful being who'll make sure that you're looked after, especially seeing you're friends with Freya. He cares a lot for his sister."

Pointing at the god, who looks as though he's cut out to please all females, I wave a finger, circling the spot he stands in the distance. "But... but he looks like he's interested in one thing only. It's not that I'm not interested in males—I just don't want to have some god trying to win my attention in that way. Besides, what would he know about anything?"

Thor places a hand on my shoulder, and my friend's reassurance works away some of the knots of apprehension. "Don't worry. He won't put a hand on you unless you want him to."

I cross my arms. "Well, that won't happen."

"Despite the obvious, he does know a lot about peace. You should fly down and meet him."

Shrugging, I realize I have nothing to lose. "I guess so." Clasping Elan's scales, I am readying myself to climb onto her bare back when Thor's voice stops me.

"Wait."

I gaze back over my shoulder.

Thor slaps his palm on his forehead. "I almost forgot." He slips his hammer into his belt and points down at his two goats, strapped to the carriage they pull, resting not far below the tip of the mountain's crest.

I let go of Elan's scales. Something large is sitting on the carriage, but I have trouble working out what it is in the dim light of the rising quarter moon.

"You're welcome!" Thor calls out. "That thing isn't light. I don't know how you've managed to haul it around. I almost had to put on my belt of strength to put it in the carriage."

Blinking, I frown before my heart thumps wildly in excitement. "It's Elan's saddle," I croon as gratitude warms my body. "I've missed that saddle. Thank you for thinking of me." Yanking on Elan's scales, I prepare to fly the short distance, and Beowulf climbs onto her back without invitation. As I look down at Thor, he seems small and lonely.

"Would you like a lift down?" I ask.

"What? You mean I get to ride a dragon?" His excitement is evident.

Elan turns on him with her teeth bared in a funny grin. *Take it easy, Thor. If you misbehave, god or no god, it may be the only time you get to ride a dragon.*

Thor grins. "I know you love me."

The Midgardian warrior offers a helping hand to Thor. "It's a fantastic experience."

Thor takes the hand offered, the muscles in his arms flexing as he pulls himself up. "And so is causing the sky to fork lightning and grumble with thunder."

"Oh, listen to him, would you?" Beowulf grunts. "You'd think he's someone special."

Elan groans under Thor's added weight. "Wow, Thor. You're heavy. It must be all those cows you eat."

"You're just jealous because I can eat more than you."

I can almost picture Elan's disagreeable face as she pushes off, carrying us to the goat carriage.

Without waiting, I jump off Elan's back and circle the carriage, studying the saddle in the dim light. Thuds sound behind me as Thor and Beowulf climb down to join me.

Taking in my excitement, Thor grins. "I had to smuggle it past my father. Fortunately in this case, he's still not up to full strength and still spends a lot of time in his room."

"Is he still getting over his prophecy from Mimir's Well?" Concern washes over me, temporarily displacing my disappointment over being banished.

"Oh, don't worry. The old man will get over that shortly. He's tough and will come back with a vengeance." Thor huffs. "It still doesn't keep him from getting annoyed and dealing out punishments."

My mouth stretches into a thin line. "I'm too aware."

Elan squats, and Thor helps me throw the large saddle over her back and secure the straps. The exhaustion from our ordeal in Muspelheim catches up with me, and lethargy creeps into my muscles, making me grateful for Thor's help. Hooking my foot in a stirrup, I grasp the edge of the saddle and heave myself up. I'm amused by how small the god of thunder looks from up here.

A thought crosses my mind. "So how did you know where I was, Thor?"

"Freya let me know. She sent me a message through Ratatoskr."

"Oh?" An image of the loving goddess flashes through my memory, unafraid to show her emotions, and her calm and collected, wanting peace and searching for the best in people. "I can't imagine her sending a message through Ratatoskr. Does she know how to send insults?"

Thor gives me an amused look. "Battle maiden, she comes up with the most interesting and disgusting messages that you wouldn't even comprehend."

My jaw drops, and my cheeks turn red when I think about whatever might be said by a love goddess to someone like Thor.

There must've been enough moonlight shining on

my face because Thor smirks. "Would you like me to tell you some?"

"No," I blurt too quickly. "Thank you. I don't need that image sparking the wrong kind of imagination. Let's go, Elan."

I breathe a sigh of relief as she pushes off and glides slowly down to the commune of angels of death, leaving Thor and Beowulf to catch up with us in the goat-drawn carriage. Having the saddle underneath me again feels good, giving me more grip and less chance of falling off her scaled back. Her scales glow in the dim light of the fire as we circle, listening to the rumbling of the carriage. When it nears the fire, Elan lands, and I climb off, waiting for Thor.

Arms wrap around me, and I gaze up in shock to find Freya embracing me.

"Thank goodness you're okay, Kara. I was so worried."

Hugging isn't my forte, but I return her embrace. A strange sense of peace fills me as I soak up the genuine concern that Freya feels for people.

"Thanks for sending your angels. I'm sorry I had to drag you into this. I didn't want Surt to get anywhere near you."

She shifts backward to study my face, clasping both of my upper arms gently. Her features are lovely, and I'm almost envious of her physique and mannerisms until I remind myself that she's a goddess. Nothing can be compared to her beauty, not even the beautiful Valkyries.

"Oh, Kara. It's because of me that you were in that mess in the first place. Besides, Surt is stupid to think he can take me as a wife."

Giving her a cheeky grin, I ask, "So does that mean that you're not going to say yes?"

One side of her face screws up with amusement. "Like I would ever say yes to that baboon. Could you imagine?" She waves a dismissive hand at me. "And that realm would be a horrible place to live. So much hatred and destruction. I couldn't do it."

"Are you going to introduce us, sis?"

Behind her shoulder stands Freyr, tall and thin with blond hair, his features similar to hers. "Is this the Valkyrie?" His eyes pass over my wingless shoulders.

Chapter Twenty-Two

Freya turns, opening a gap to let her brother into our small circle. "Of course. Why wouldn't I introduce you to her? This is Kara. Kara, this is Freyr, my brother."

Freyr moves quickly, clasping my hand and raising the back to his mouth, dusting a kiss on my skin. "And to what do I owe the pleasure of meeting such a beautiful woman?" Sensual tones filled with invitation lace his voice. The question is a greeting that doesn't expect an answer.

Heat rushes to my cheeks, which burn under his intense gaze, and I face away to hide my response. Sexuality and peace simply seep from him, just like his sister.

"I can't wait to take you with me to Alfheim." Sensual fingers coax my chin softly, directing my gaze back to his sweet smile. "You'll be under my protection and guidance, and I'll do everything in my power to make sure you're looked after."

Not knowing how to react or what to say, I gently pry my hand from his touch and look at Beowulf, almost begging for help.

The Midgardian warrior's eyes cut through my insecurity, and other than when I first saw him in Muspelheim, I've never been so glad to hear the warrior's boisterous voice. "Oh, Freya. It's so good to see you again. I'm at your service to use as you please as long as you grace me with your presence."

The words sound so foreign from the coarse warrior's mouth, and I have to stifle a laugh, especially when he bends at the waist in a bow, Freya's hand clasped in his.

"May I wash your feet or something else of more importance?" Beowulf's voice is laced with seduction, and I cringe, not so sure he's bringing me the distraction I want.

Freya's chuckle sounds like finely tuned bells chiming. Touching her loose hand to her heart, she gracefully pulls her hand out of Beowulf's grasp.

"Why, I'm flattered, Beowulf, but you aren't one of my warriors."

Disappointment flashes across his face. With eyes downcast, he straightens.

Freya clasps his chin and lifts it, looking into his

blue eyes. "But if you play your cards right while you're alive, perhaps you will eventually be one of my warriors."

Beowulf almost melts in front of Freya, his expression only changing when he's interrupted by Thor.

"Beowulf, you're a powerful, strong warrior, and I would hate to see your talents wasted. Perhaps when you die, you can come to Valhalla to serve by my side." Thor studies Beowulf's besotted face ogling Freya, and I think I see hurt showing in his eyes. "I thought that was your plan."

Beowulf makes an obvious effort to pry his eyes off the beautiful goddess to speak directly to Thor. "I don't see why I can't have both." Within seconds, his eyes return to Freya as he retakes her hand like a knight addressing his princess.

Freya chuckles, softly removing her hand again. "Then you would be an original first. Anyway, my darling Beowulf, we're here for Kara and her protection since Odin has banished her from Asgard." Smoothly, she turns to her brother. "Now, Freyr"— her stern eyes focus on him—"you must look after Kara and help her find a good teacher of magic without making unwanted passes at her."

Freyr affectionately hugs his sister around the shoulders, fixing her with innocent eyes. "I would never."

She raises an eyebrow at him. "You and I both know that you would. This isn't why I've put Kara into your care."

My attention flicks from one to the other, finishing on Elan, my eyes pleading. "Help me," I whisper.

Elan tilts her head to one side, pretending to look thoughtful. *Now, what would Naga say about it?* She lifts her talons and taps her temple several times. *Oh yes, he would say that you're of breeding age and in genuine need of finding a mate before you get too old.*

I glower at her. "Elan!" I cry in shock, causing everyone's eyes to fix on me, including the angels of death. Once again, my cheeks redden even though I know Elan didn't send that message to the rest of the group.

She grins, showing off her vicious smile.

Thor clears his throat, and I'm glad for the interruption. "I was afraid this might happen." He studies Freyr, his expression serious, almost like a protective father's. "As Freya said, you aren't to touch her unless she allows it."

The sensual god looks slightly offended, although unconvincingly.

Thor ignores him and continues, "Just as I thought. For this reason, I've called for one of her friends to go with her to Alfheim also."

My heart skips a beat, surging with excitement, and I want to hug my leader.

"This friend is probably a better suit for you and your realm in their attitude." Thor adjusts his hammer into a more comfortable position. "A Valkyrie whose heart is full of peace, love, and understanding, always wanting to see the good in people. And with her is her dragon, who carries the same beliefs."

The knowledge Thor holds of my friends surprises me. I know he can only be talking about one Valkyrie and her bonded dragon.

A soft voice sounds just behind me, almost a whisper. "Listen to that. He's saying such nice things about Naga."

Turning, I find Eir hugging Naga around the neck. I start briefly, not having realized they were there. They were so silent, sneaking up on me.

"Eir. I'm so glad to see you." Relieved, I wrap my arms around her neck and stroke Naga's blue cheek, smiling when the dragon leans into my hand. "You're so quiet. I didn't hear you two sneak up."

Eir shrugs. "We've perfected the art of walking without being heard—well, most of the time. It was easy while you were distracted. You probably heard us but ignored the sound."

I squeeze her hand, whispering, "Thank you. I'm

ecstatic to have a friend accompanying me this time." Naga catches my eyes with his big blue ones. "Two friends," I correct myself.

Eir leans to one side. "I wouldn't be surprised if Odin banishes me also for going with you." Catching my worried gaze, she shrugs. "It's something we'll tackle together. Besides, I want to come. When would I ever say no to learning more about peaceful magic?"

I chuckle. "Never."

Naga nudges me from the side with his nose. *Naga's excited to be coming. Naga has heard much about this land.*

I frown. "Oh. What's that?"

Naga has heard that there are peaceful dragons somewhere in one of these realms. Perhaps this is the place. Naga would like to meet friendly dragons, not like these dragons that want to breathe fire and fight all the time. His gaze turns to Elan. *Like the emperor dragons.*

The scales between Elan's eyes push together in a frown. *Naga, my breed is nothing compared to the dragon we ran into in Muspelheim. That dragon was na-a-asty!*

Naga's eyes widen.

"That's true," I say. "But that dragon remains in Muspelheim. It wouldn't be able to survive anywhere else. It would destroy everything it touched."

I catch Eir's shocked expression.

"It's a story I'll tell you on our travels," I say. "I'm glad to have you come with us, Naga. I couldn't think of any better companions than you two."

Catching Thor's attention, I say, "If you manage to speak to your father, please explain that I'm sorry. I didn't mean to set Loki free, and I'll do my best to bring him back. Asgard is my home. It holds all my friends and favorite gods. I'll always stand by and protect them."

Thor places a hand on my upper arm. "I'll do my best. You know I will, Kara. I want you back in Asgard. I have a lot more planned for you, and I'm not going to give up on you yet. I can see your loyalty even if my stubborn father can't."

I pull away from Thor's intense gaze and connect with the smiling blond god. Freyr stares at both Eir and me alternately for several moments, wearing a broad smirk.

I'm not sure if I want to cringe or be happy.

"Shall we get started?" the blond god asks.

My expression doesn't change.

He seems to realize my apprehension and inclines his head. "Do not worry, battle maidens. I'll do as instructed. I'll protect you and lead you through my realm. I think you'll find my followers very accommodating." He holds out one hand as an invitation.

Without grasping his hand, I step forward hesitantly. "Okay. Let's do this. I'm keen to expand my magic."

THE END

Hoodwinked: Book 4 Released January, 2021

If you enjoyed Entrapment, please take a few minutes and leave a review on Amazon. Thank you. Reviews help authors.

ACKNOWLEDGMENTS

Thank you to all of the creators of literature and websites who have spent time writing about Norse Mythology. Even though at times there has been contradicting information, it has been an interesting study. After all, of course a goat produces mead, and a dragon gnaws at the roots of the Yggdrasil, unhindered, threatening the existence of the nine realms attached to the world tree. Plus, there are many other "believable" tales told.

Norse mythology is such an impressive set of tales that I have incorporated some and invented others to create Kara and Elan's story.

I am touched by the enormous amount of support I have received from my immediate family. My husband has been a helpful first reader and, at times, been an excellent motivator, with hints of ideas to help me through the blanks. The support from my three sons has also been overwhelming. They have spent years putting up with my head in the clouds, thinking about the next plot twist or story, along with many hours spent working on my books and keeping in touch with my readers.

A big thank you to my extended family, who support me being a book enthusiast.

A huge thank you to my editor, Kelly Reed, her editing and writing tips, and my Proofreader, Irene S, for picking up the things we missed.

Thank you to all of my readers who have loved my work, and continue to read my stories.

BOOKS BY KATRINA COPE

Pre-Teen Books

The Sanctum Series

JAYDEN'S CYBERMOUNTAIN

SCARLET'S ESCAPE

TAYLOR'S PLIGHT

ERIC & THE BLACK AXES

ADRIANNA'S SURGE

~~~~~

Young Adult Urban Fantasy

Afterlife Series

FLEDGLING

THE TAKING

ANGELIC RETRIBUTION

DIVIDED PATHS

TRUTH HUNTER

Afterlife Novelette

THE GATEKEEPER

~~~~~

Young Adult Urban Paranormal Fantasy

HOODWINKED

ABOUT THE AUTHOR

Katrina is a best-selling author of young adult fantasy and middle grade/tween novels. Her novels incorporate action, heart and an intriguing plot.

She resides in Queensland, Australia. Her three teenage boys and husband for over twenty years treat her like a princess. Unfortunately though, this princess still has to do domestic chores.

From a very young age, she has been a very creative person and has spent many years travelling the world and observing many different personalities and cultures. Her favourite personalities have been the strange ones, yet the ones under the radar also hold a place in her heart.

Katrina's online home is at www.katrinacopebooks.com

You can connect with Katrina on:

Facebook Group